DARK MOONS RISING ON A STARLESS NIGHT

MAME BOUGOUMA DIENE

CLASH

TABLE OF CONTENTS

FISTULAS

CHAPTER 1

Dr. Salio Sanogo picked up the small scalpel from the table. He dipped it in rubbing alcohol before turning to the young girl lying unconscious on the operating table, and sliced the mangled skin covering her vagina.

He preformed this operation numerous times inside his clinic in Seledougou. The girl had Type III FGM, infibulation. The edges of her vulva had been almost completely stitched together to prevent intercourse. She could never pee properly and it was badly infected. She had run away from her village, and stumbled upon him somehow. How she'd managed to find them through the pain was beyond him.

Dr. Salio knew first hand that good people attracted bad things in the way breasts attract idiots. Little girls could be mischievous, if not downright evil in their efforts to redirect chaos, but youth was an excuse for itself, and, ready to carefully draw the young woman's clitoris out from under the trauma inflicted on her, he also knew that none so young could have earned this through any kind of guilt, past or future.

"Stephanie, see how the excision was performed all the way up here, but she was sewn way down to here?" Dr. Salio asked the young Belgian intern, as he finished slicing the skin open.

"That's why she had difficulty peeing?"

"Yes. The hole is too small, much too small, so the urine pushed out through the skin."

"Can you help her, Doctor?"

"Yes, we're lucky, look," he said pulling apart the undamaged lips under the stitching. "It didn't mutilate her organ per se, it's almost intact, and see," he opened the scar tissue entirely, "her clitoris is still right here, all we have to do is pull a little..." he turned to the nurse standing by the bed, adjusting the girl's IV drip. "Satou, check that she is still sedated enough, we only need thirty minutes."

"We've already given her all the sedatives we could, doctor." Nurse Aïssatou responded, "her body rejects them; you will have to be quick."

It wasn't her body rejecting the sedatives, it was her brain. She wanted this done, she needed this done, but all the same she hated anything foreign done to her. Again. She would need a lot of care, and some time away, to rest and for no one to find her.

He drew a deep breath, staring through the mosquito net surrounding the table at the slightly cracked paint on the ceiling, and the tiny dried bloodstains on the wall, still holding little bits of wings and limbs from smashed bugs, wiped his forehead, and proceeded to drawing out the young girl's clitoris out, a thousandth of an inch at a time. Thirty minutes stretched into eternity.

And then it was over.

"We're done here, hé." Salio said, handing the scalpel to Stephanie. "Satou can you please clean the blood, and have her covered. Let her rest, when she recovers have Stephanie check on her every two hours for the next..."

"Doctor! Doctor!" A young boy barged into the clinic shouting, earning a grunt from the young girl resting from the surgery, "The Unwomen are here! The Unwomen are here!"

The who...

"You mean the U.N Women Amadou?"

"Yes Doctor," he grinned, scratching the back of his head. "The UN women. And they have cameras and a truck for you!"

For me...

Work was starting to get to him. He had promised them an

interview, but no one had said anything about cameras and a truck.

"Well, they do fund part of the clinic...Stephanie, check on her every two hours for the next day, keep her hydrated. I have to head for Bamako tomorrow, a presentation at Save the Children, but I'll back in forty-eight hours. Satou, think you can handle the clinic without me?"

"Sure Doc. You go and raise the funding we need, and have yourself a proper steak and bed, then come back here, hé? We have work to do."

"Yes, Nurse Diawara," he said, snapping a smart salute and earning a frown, and walked out of the clinic behind Amadou.

"So, you can fix the clitoris?" the CNN reporter asked, sitting across from him on a stool, the cameras behind him catching a shot of Salio while showing just enough of the village's emaciated cows' ribs, walking through the dusty village square. The lights blinded him. He could hardly see the man, drowned in more light than the village used in a year.

"Absolutely," Dr. Salio answered.

"But it's cut, isn't it? Isn't it...gone?"

"That's a common misconception. The clitoris is in fact much, much larger than you think. The erectile tissue wraps around most of the pelvic area, so we make sure we open the scar tissue carefully and draw some of it out. It's a forty-five minute procedure at most. With a 95% success rate."

"Wow! That's gotta be quite a feeling, huh?"

"Yes," Dr. Salio answered coldly. It was odd being here, answering this foreign man's poverty porn questions, commenting on all these women's pain. It was almost uncomfortable, but many victims didn't want to be seen, and refused to comment. And why would they?. It wasn't his place but it was all he knew.

"And...the delicate question...what of...*sensation*, do the women you perform on, actually find pleasure again in their intimate life?"

"Well. First we are trying to restore dignity to the women who have been mutilated, and heal wounds and infections that they have developed since. That is very important. Now, of course the sexual aspect is a concern as well, but that is, as it were, in the hands of God. But we are successful in slightly over 50% of the cases."

"You're doing an amazing work, doctor."

"Thank you."

"And considering the resources…"

"Yes, the procedure costs 450 euros in Paris, but we get by with 150 including post-surgical care here, it triples our efficiency."

"You are treating a lot of women here. Would you say you are facing an epidemic of Female Genital Mutilation in the region?"

"People like to come to Africa and throw the word epidemic around don't they?" he said, earning a second frown for the day. "But I was born a few miles south of here, and things were much worse then."

"Yes. That's why you studied abroad…"

"Yes, obstetrics and then clitoroplasty with Dr. Hannes Sigur-jónsson in Sweden…"

"And I have been led to understand that your own sister was a victim of FGM and…"

Dr. Salio stood up. "Look, with your army fatigues and mani-cured hair. This isn't the next thing for you to talk about over brunch. These are real people, and I'm not about to peddle my life for your ratings and a couple hundred bucks. I'll work for free. Hear me, Yankee boy?"

The reporter was a pro. He blinked. Twice, and flashed pearly teeth at him. Dr. Salio turned his back on him, disgusted.

"To hell with you and your network," he said, and walked away.

———

There were very few hyenas this far south, but sometimes they had too little carcasses to fight over. Two hyenas were a blur of grey and black stripes, swarming over a dead buffalo, its eyes already gone, the hide drying against bones, the lustrous black traded for a thick coat of flies.

The flies rose in a cloud, throwing themselves at the exposed rot, biting each other more often than not.

They might as well eat themselves. Hyena's gotta taste better than that, Doctor Salio thought, looking out the window at the feast fading behind the bus, and the swathes of grass, still green from the rainy season. How subtly the landscape changed from the arid cliffs around Bamako to the gently rolling plains and thin forests further south always amazed him, but he recognized the same greed in the hyenas that he did in people—there was little amazement in that.

"What are you looking at so hard?" an amused voice asked besides him.

He turned to find an older woman, her head wrapped in green and pink with a colorful blue and brown dress bearing an effigy of president IBK, staring at him hungrily.

"Handsome man like you, and sharp dresser too! What you doing here? You with an NGO?"

"I'm a doctor, and I wasn't looking at anything really. Just… well, thinking about things…"

"Heeeeey! Doctor, hé? I knew I had me a catch! I'm going to Fakola, I cook a good tinani, you get hungry, you come see me, hé?"

"That sounds good, hé. But I'm headed for Seledougou."

"Tsk!" she snapped with her tongue against her pallet, pulling away from him, a severe look in her eyes. "Why you wanna go there? Harami! That place is cursed. Young man, you smart doctor and all, you should know better."

———

He chuckled. The village she meant was further east of his, but if that slimeball reporter had wanted to see an epidemic he should have visited them. FGM had decimated the village. The women couldn't deliver; improvised C-sections had made things worse. The youth had gone; all there was left were some aging couples and a few young women, probably too sick to leave. There was no curse, but that kind of evil would leave a taint anywhere.

"There is no curse, auntie."

"All their babies are born dead they say. I have heard this from people I trust."

"Not all of them, some of the children come to our village for small items sometimes, but they have a lot of stillborn."

"And it never rains."

He barked a laugh. "Come on now. Those are rumors, hé. The desert is far north. We are a few miles away and we get rain, not very much but enough. I hear their wells are very dry and the little water they get isn't good. Something must be wrong with the water table, pollutants or something. Makes them sick and kills the babies. There is always an explanation."

She looked him up and down with her lips twisted, shaking her head as if watching a simpleton yanking on his noodle, before turning away and saying, "Dr. Boy. The curse *is* the explanation."

Doctor Salio stepped out of the bus in the middle of Seledougou's small square. He picked up his briefcase and walked towards Djibril Diallo's little shop for some bread before heading back to the clinic.

Salio walked inside the shop. "Tonton," Dr. Salio said, addressing Djibril, "I'll take a couple of loaves of bread, hé, and a can of tuna."

"Coming right up Doctor." Djibril said, handing over two dusty loaves. "That'll be 125 francs for you. Each. That's 750 for the tuna."

Dr. Salio was exhausted, and wanted nothing more than head to his house and rest, but he was also hungry, and Djibril had to be kidding. "Djibril. 125CFA for your rancid bread? Really? Where you keep the good stuff, hé? Get me the fresh bread now."

"The fresh...hahaha!" Djibril laughed at Salio. "Mamadou!" he called at his son. "You gotta hear this!"

Mamadou came running bare chested out of the back of the small boutique cluttered with boxes of Algerian imitation snickers bars and juices, caramels, cans of canned milk, matchboxes, tang and a thousand-thousand cubes of chicken broth.

His father slapped him on the back. "Guess what The Swede wants...Fresh bread!"

The joke was lost on the boy who smiled and walked back to his work.

"Fresh bread, hé?" Djibril said. "I'll bake it after I harvest the fields of wheat just west of here! Hahaha! What did you ask for in Sweden? Foutou Plantain? It's 125 each."

"Bah, you're lucky you're the only one with any bread at all," Dr. Salio said, handing him the money, snatching the two loaves and walked towards the clinic.

CHAPTER 2

There was a commotion in front of the clinic. It happened sometimes. Everybody still wasn't happy about the doctor's work. Traditions run deep, even foul ones, especially foul ones.

The young girl should be healing by now, but he had to make sure the tip didn't retract or he'd have to start again. There weren't as many cases as there used to be, still too many, but back then there wouldn't have been a doctor to do his job, either. That poor chump would have got murdered, or ran out in his birthday suit. Groups of villagers from neighboring hamlets would come threaten him, but this was different, he recognized most of the villagers' voices screaming at his nurse, and Aissatou's shouting louder than most.

"Kill them!" A villager yelled, shaking his fist.

"You give them to us you hear!" another echoed.

"Kumbi, they had some friends with them! Catch them! Round them all up!"

"You try to get near these children and I'll tell everybody your dirty secret Moctar Cissé!" Nurse Aissatou yelled to the third heckler as Salio shoved his way through the crowd.

She had two terrified children he didn't recognize trying to hide behind her gown, crying softly, their eyes wide with terror, little drops of mucus falling from their nose on her robe, while she waved a large stick at the men gathered in front of her.

"What the hell is going on here?!" Dr. Salio screamed, quieting most of the crowd.

"Devils!" someone screamed.

Moctar approached him. "They're from the cursed village. I never let them touch me, hé! They touched my child, they will infect her. She will grow two like them. Give them to us. We must kill them!"

Approving grunts came from the crowd. He turned towards Aissatou and the children. "What is he talking about?!"

She came closer, waving the stick, the children hanging to her with their fists covered in tears and slime, and leaned over and whispered in his ear. "The kids, there's something wrong with…"

He pulled back. "Really?! Are you sure?!"

She nodded.

"The two of them!"

She nodded again, looking him in the eye.

He paused. *That's impossible, both of those kids?* He turned to the others. "Look, You know me, I have never lied to you, and I wouldn't now." He earned a few grunts. "This is not a curse," he earned a few stares, "and if it's a curse it is not contagious, I have seen this before."

He felt the tension loosen a little, but not enough.

"Bring me the other children," Dr. Salio said. "I will examine them. We will talk afterwards."

"I trust you Doctor Salio." Moctar said shaking his finger at him, "You've done good here. But I am staying close to my little girl. If anything happens I will kill those children myself, and don't get in my way."

Dr. Salio put out his cigarette, shaking his head and looking at the three boys and two girls chewing on bread and tuna sandwiches, sometimes staring at the window or door with a hint of their previous panic. It had been a long day's ride, but nothing had prepared him for this. Nothing.

"This makes no sense," Doctor Salio said. "These kids have both genitalia, all five of them, Satou, both, a penis, and…and right there! A slit, labia and all, where the testicles rest." Doctor Salio said "I don't know what to tell the people. How did they find out anyway? It's not that obvious, hé."

"Moctar's daughter saw one of the girls peeing standing up, and ran to her father, those two made it here before the villagers could catch them. Good thing too," Nurse Aissatou said.

"They're usually very discreet."

"Now we know why."

"Yeah, but…" he couldn't wrap his mind around it. "What am I gonna tell those people? And what is going on over there? The stillborn and this? What is in that water?!"

"You tell them what you've told them before, and what you've been mumbling under your breath for the better part of an hour. That you've seen this before, and that you're heading there to investigate."

"But I have *never* seen this before!" he started to yell, but held back, seeing the kids turning to him, ready to run for the door. "I mean…I have seen hermaphrodites before, but *no one* has ever seen this before…"

She slapped him across the face. "Get a hold of yourself." She said angrily. "Get a hold of yourself or these kids are dead. Here, have a cigarette. Steady your nerves. You know how to do this, drown them with words like the NGOs do. I don't care. Convince them."

The children were safely behind him in Aissatou's arms while he spoke to the villagers. The tension had abated, as it would after a couple of hours of anticlimax, but they had been a lifetime for him and the children. He had rehearsed every word before stepping out.

"I will be back in a week with answers. I know what I'm doing. Nurse Diawara will hold the clinic; she's called four of her cousins to help. Everything will be taken care of."

It had been easier than he'd thought. The passion for murder burns brightly, but it burns fast. And in spite of what they knew, they had to look at terrified children, and thankfully a doctor who had helped cure most of them free of charge for almost two years.

"Hé! You one foolish doctor." Moctar said, his dark skinned face both incredulous and full of contempt, "But maybe it's better if you go. They will never let you leave."

"They trust their children to come here and back, I'm sure they know gratitude just as we do, and a free doctor to boot. You know exactly what I mean," Dr. Salio said.

"That village is cursed Dr. Salio."

"It doesn't rain there."

"Well, it doesn't rain that much here either."

"Have it your way," "Moctar said, "but if you don't return we won't come looking for you. That place is wrong, Salio. It has been for years, you weren't here. We are happy you've returned, but perhaps you should remember where you are."

Dr. Salio smiled and looked at the kids. They smiled weakly still glancing nervously at the villagers. They looked healthier than the children of Seledougou in fact, their clothes had seen a lot of needles, no second-hand Adidas or baseball hats, but they were no guiltier than the teenagers he operated on.

"I know exactly where I am, and that's why I'm going there. These people need help, same as these girls in there." He said pointing at the clinic. "I'll be back and it will all brush over. Thank you for trusting me."

"You know doctor, everything can't be learned, some things you can only feel."

"I feel good about this."

CHAPTER 3

Dr. Salio tightened his bag against his back and walked up to Aissatou. The village turned to forest behind her. He couldn't see much into the trees, but the children would know all the shortcuts.

"How fast are your cousins gonna be here?"

"Tomorrow morning. They're useless around the lab but they're built like gorillas."

"Good, have them sleep in the lab, keep the girls safe, hé. If other villages hear of this, four won't be too many. "

She nodded, glancing at the villagers.

He hugged her and let the children grab his hands. They looked up at him giggling, whispering into each other's ears and fidgeting.

"Alright kids. Who's showing me the way?"

They looked at each other, and ran off into the forest waving at him to follow.

Dr. Salio had forgotten how much the forest changed, even so near his village. He knew where and when every bush would appear on the way back from Bamako, but every patch of forest hid an entire world, and even this near, the same plants changed already. He knew nothing about plants, but apparently neither did the children. He would ask for a name, and they would shrug and run along.

There was no path either, but the same way the bus ride was no mystery to him, neither were the thickets and rocks to the kids. Good thing they were in the driver's seat. He would be lost by now.

"Hey! Not so fast, I'm an old man, you know?" Dr. Salio said, calling after the children.

"Hey. Slow down for grandpa. His old bones are letting go." Dr. Salio heard one of the older boys say to one of the girls under his breath as to not offend him.

"My old bones are just fine," he replied.

The cocky boy hid behind the little girl he was trying to impress, and Dr. Salio laughed.

They followed a small stream for a few hundred yards that shrunk to a trickle in a small clearing, bubbling between roots and disappearing completely.

That's when the children stopped.

Something had changed in the forest. He couldn't tell what, but he wasn't in the same place anymore. Perhaps the branches were more crooked and the grass a sicklier green. Perhaps, but this wasn't the same forest, or if it was…

It's the breeze. It stopped once we crossed the clearing.

The forest smelled stronger, without the draft carrying the sappy underbrush away, each plant seemed to have a personality of its own, all mingling in a puff of decaying leaves and stagnant ponds.

There was always someone or something in a forest to hear the tree fall, it might be the animals hit by the tree, it might be the birds taking off a fraction of a second before it collapsed, but no one would have heard it here. There wasn't a sound, not a hint of whooshing through the branches, not a chirp or buzzing.

The children put a finger to their lips. Listening intently to the sounds in the forest they'd left behind.

When nothing gave after a few minutes, they relaxed, staring at him their eyes wet with tears, and rushed to hug him.

"Thank you, Doctor." The cocky little boy said, burying his face into his thigh.

"Thank you. Thank you. Thank you. Thank you." Two more whispered.

"They were going to kill us Doctor. Please don't tell our mothers. Please. Or they will kill us."

"They might give you a good spanking." Dr. Salio said, shaking his finger at them in mock scolding, "But you deserve it, hé. You should be more careful, you know to be careful."

They nodded at him.

Dr. Salio broke a little, looking into their earnest eyes, it was so easy to forget there was anything different about them, and why would he even remember that? They were children.

"We´re almost there Mr. Doctor. And no one is following us." One of the little girls said, smiling.

So that's what that was about. Those kids know their stuff.

"Alright then, let's get going, but easy, hé! You're safe now. No need to run."

They giggled, and something about old bones came up again, but he ignored it, following them into the pungent microcosm.

They weren't as close as he'd thought, but something was happening to the forest. The trees seemed to lose their sap, it oozed and bubbled through holes in the bark, dripping white, translucent and sticky along the trunks.

It was true for the leaves and plants too. Their inner fluids staining the stems and leaves with reddish brown blotches.

His gourd was empty, and the little rivulet had never bubbled out again. The few fruit on the branches looked appetizing, and he recognized a ripened ackee, a little small, but nonetheless, and he was thirsty.

I really got to get used to local water again.

He'd drank only bottled or boiled water for two years. Maybe he really was The Swede.

He ripped the pinkish-red fruit from the tree. On closer inspection, most of the thick skin was brown, but the exposed fruit seeds were a rich dark black, and the milky arils smelled fresh.

He pulled it out and took a bite. The sweet juice trickled down his throat. It had been a long time since he'd had ackee fresh off the tree. It teased a smile from his mother, a reprieve from his father, a giggle from his sister in his mind, and a tear from his eye.

He'd been so young.

By the time he took a bite out of the second pulp it had turned rotten and dry. He doubled over, spitting ashy bits of pulp from his mouth, trying to clear his itchy throat and dry heaving on the side of the tree.

"You ok, Mr. Doctor?" one of the two girls asked.

He looked aside to see the children staring at him anxiously. He pulled himself up, coughed one last time and wiped the spittle off his lips with his sleeve.

"How do you..." he started, but stopped and asked instead "What do you eat?"

The children looked at each other confused. No one had asked them that before.

One of the boys spoke up. "No Dr. Sir. No one eats anything from the forest. We only eat from the Mother Tree. You'll see. We are very close now. Don't worry."

———

"We do not know you," a thick, burly man told Dr. Salio, holding a small lance and what looked like a rusty machine gun under the torches, behind his back.

"Yes," said another man, as large as the first. "You are not allowed near the Mother Tree without the Tree Mothers' approval."

"But I can see the tree from here." Doctor Salio answered.

The branches on the baobab stood higher and thicker than any tree he had ever seen. Even behind the hill where the pathway curved towards the village he could see it.

"Yes you can," one of the guards retorted "She is a very special tree, if it wasn't night time already you would have noticed her for miles. Now wait here. We will see to the children. We will be back soon."

The two men turned away, taking the children waving him goodbye, by the hand. His heart skipped a beat. Funny what children do to you, even in the space of a few hours.

The night was humid and the air stale. He could make out

drums beating a procession somewhere behind the bend, but there were still no sounds otherwise.

The three men left guarding him were massive. He couldn't tell their age, there was something strangely healthy about them, just as in the kids. Much healthier than anyone in his own village, or the surrounding villages. *Do they also have two organs?* Two of the men had horizontal scars on their stomach, but the third was the oddest. His stomach was hugely inflated, as if he had kwashiorkor; his muscles held a lot of fatty tissue, his face was pudgy and the fingers wrapped around his spear looked like bratwursts.

He reeked of a strong hormonal stench. Dr. Salio had to turn his head slightly, but without a draft, it was all he could do not to throw up. If the other two noticed they didn't show. *Probably used to it.*

The drums kept rolling slowly. There was something mournful to it, but there were no chants, only the rolling beat, the guards' torches and the man's stink.

Lights shone against the side of the hill with the elongated shadows of the other guards returning.

"The Tree Mothers will see you. Follow us."

———

Bam-Bam-Bam...Bam,Bam-Bam-Bam...Bam-Bam,Bam-Bam-Bam...Bam...

"What is happening here?" Doctor Salio asked.

The procession he'd heard had stopped by the roots of the baobab. Even after seeing its branches he hadn't expected this. There were more people in the village than he thought. The dancing flames made it hard to count, especially in the moonless night, but however many they were, they were dwarfed by the hulking plant.

It stretched further around than he could see. Larger and taller than the hill. The roots the people gathered around reached to their stomachs. The trunk was thick and gnarly, six-foot thick branches growing ten feet from the ground spread up in a nappy crown, giving the behemoth the look of an hourglass. *With enough sand to account for all the time in the world.* It must have been as old as the pyramids.

They passed a small object wrapped in a white shroud from the back to the front, and handed it to a man, who held it up in the air. The shroud had the vague shape of a newborn, but sickly small and premature.

There was nothing special about the man holding the child, no ritualistic attire of any kind, he had a fresh scar on his stomach, and he didn't chant, he turned around and stepped between the roots, knelt with the small child, and the drums stopped.

His guards looked at the procession and said nothing. The fat one began to weep quietly.

"If the Tree Mothers wish to tell you, they will."

They walked away from the gathering and up a pathway curving onto a large open space, lined with dried out bushes around it and a path of packed dirt leading to a large, circular mud hut painted bright blue, with a straw covered dome.

Voices rang inside. He recognized some of the children he'd accompanied, but there were other voices as well. More mature and melodic, and shadows dancing along the walls that looked like women.

The guards stopped and let him pass.

"Go in. The Tree Mothers have asked for you alone."

"Thanks," Dr. Salio answered, walking up to the strings of Koris barring the door.

He pushed them away and walked in.

The shadows were women. Ten stunning women, sitting bare-chested in the center of a carpet covered room, hugging the children, and weeping into their hair.

"I can't wait to punish you," one of them said, tickling one of the little girls. "Just because it means you are here and you are safe."

She noticed Dr. Sanogo and stood up, walking towards him.

She had a light blue saran wrapped around her slim waste and long legs, almost to her perfect bare feet. She wore nothing on top, except a necklace of kori shells resting between her pear shaped breasts. She swayed as she walked, closing hypnotic greyish eyes on him, and smiling.

Mashallah!

She caught his hands in hers.

"Thank you so much," she said, her smile concealing a tear. "They are usually here by the afternoon. We were so worried."

"It's normal," he said, finding it difficult to think. "They are children."

"No it's not. They told us what you have done, doctor. It was very brave. Other villages have killed our children before, and those who try to protect them." She turned to look at the children fondly. "But we will punish them. Scaring us like this." Outside the drums picked up again, and the great tree's branches creaked. "I am Aisha. Welcome to Kalakoro."

CHAPTER 4

"Wake up Doctor!"

"Wake up, it is morning!"

"Yes, Doctor, we brought you breakfast!"

Salio tried to stick his ears to his pillow but woke up as one of the children climbed on his back and shook him by the shoulders.

They smiled at him, with the sun breaking through the window in a mud hut adjacent to the larger blue one where he'd met the Tree Mothers. They'd offered him fresh fruit and some water and shown him to rest. He'd passed out almost immediately.

The children had brought him more of the fruit.

"Your famous Mother Tree fruit, hé?" he asked hitting one of them with his pillow.

"Yes doctor! It's the best."

"That's not baobab fruit," he said, looking at the crop.

But again the children shrugged.

He couldn't remember what the fruit had tasted like, he'd been too tired to, and couldn't get his mind off Aisha.

The fruit looked like an odd cross between a banana, a mushroom, and a slug. Long, with a thick tip, and splitting in two thinner strands at the bottom. Peeled, it appeared to have the consistency and fluffiness of an orange. He'd never seen anything like it before. He picked it up, and bit off the mushroom tip.

It was juicier than pineapple, fresher than watermelon, but

sweet and sour like grapefruit. It had the consistency of a banana, but much richer, as if he was eating sweet tofu.

He was getting his vitamins, carbs, fat and protein at the same time. And he was already feeling full.

No wonder they're all so fit. If someone found out about this they'd make a killing. Forget quinoa, this thing is a miracle.

He took another bite, and couldn't chew his way through all of it. "Wow, can't finish this, kids. Gonna have to take a break. Now off with you, it's grown-up time."

Aisha chose that moment to walk in, the kids running outside passed her. "Glad you're rested," she said.

He paused while thinking of his next words. "I am. Thanks. That fruit. It's very good."

She smiled. "Yes, but have some water. Don't worry, all the rumors about this place aren't true. The water is better here than where you live."

"I heard it never rained."

She laughed. "We don't have much water that is true, or much game in the forest, but the little we have is very clean, and you've tasted our fruit."

"It's amazing. What do you call it?"

"We don't have a name for it. What would be the point? It only grows here." She looked outside into the sunlight. "I have things to attend to, but I will see you tonight. Walk around the village, you'll find the people here are friendly."

"I'll do that. But I really want to talk to you about…"

"Tonight," she said walking up to him and resting a hand on his chest, smiling mischievously. "Today you learn about where you are."

Dr. Salio didn't know if the people of Kalakoro were friendly, but they were up front. A woman had thanked him for returning the kids, but also berated him for not doing so sooner; a man had asked him if he was here to steal their fruit. Now a third stomped in his direction, grinning and hulking, the same size and build the guards had been the previous night, and the man he had met earlier.

"I hear you're a doctor man, is that true?"

"Yes." Dr. Salio said, handing out his hand. "Salio Sanogo."

The man hesitated. "Malik Kadio, call me Kadio,"

"Nice to meet you Kadio. You have a strong handshake."

"Ha! Yes, well, that is my problem, my hand you see."

He opened his left hand. A large cut ran across its palm. It didn't look infected but it needed some stitching.

"That's a pretty deep cut. It's gonna need some stitching."

"Stitching?"

"I need to sow it up, needles and threads."

"Yes!" the man said slapping him on the shoulder. "Seen some people do it who don't know a needle from a thread, it looks awful."

They walked towards his hut, covered in shade by one of the tree's branches.

That tree is ridiculous. No wonder there's hardly any water, maybe the roots purify whatever it doesn't drain...

He'd been wrong last night. The night might have been moonless, but the trees branches covered half the village in shade. Roughly fifty huts never saw the light of day, and having been built around the beast, it would take thirty minutes to make it halfway across the village.

Kadio waved at a man with the same condition as the bloated guard. He wasn't as big but his stomach distended visibly, and he walked with his back arched backwards, having difficulty handling his weight. A tall, full-figured woman with her head wrapped in red and brown helped him walk towards their hut in the shade of a thick branch holding fruit that lay scattered around, and picked one up before helping him in.

"I saw someone like that yesterday," Doctor Salio said. "What's his problem?"

Kadio shrugged. "He is pregnant."

"What?"

Kadio raised a hand, ending the conversation. "Tradition. The Tree Mothers will explain."

Tradition?

Kadio's wife stepped out of the house as they walked in. She was as tall as Dr. Salio, a few inches shorter than her husband, with broad shoulders and a strong build, large breasts and broad hips, and fit, just like all the other women, or anybody he'd seen so far.

"See?" she addressed her husband reprovingly. "I told you he was a doctor."

She turned to Salio. "He wouldn't believe me. Said no one had come for years and certainly not a doctor. Make his hand right, yes? But sting him a little for me."

Dr. Salio laughed. "Well it's not very deontological but I'm sure we can find an arrangement."

She smiled and shook her head at her husband. "See? Big words. Try to learn a few while he fixes you."

After tending to Kadio's hand, and having some more fruit, Dr. Salio found that he was still exhausted from the previous day's hike, and napped inside the hut for a few hours. As he drifted to sleep he reflected on the easily welcoming people of Kalakoro. Sure, he had returned the kids and now sown up one of the villagers, but he had no doubt that lest someone came to steal their fruit, they would be just as welcoming.

*They don't deserve all the trash talked about them...*was his last thought as he fell asleep.

...Except for the kids, and the stillborn...

The thought woke him up and he rose from the small bed he'd fallen asleep on with a jolt.

Kadio was sitting in a corner looking at his hand. "You up doctor? You did a great job. Hardly felt a thing. Will tell the wife you stung me good, though."

"You're welcome. Least I can do. Thanks for the nap, I really needed that."

"Sure doctor. See you tomorrow."

Dr. Salio stepped out into the early evening sun, picked up a small fruit, unpeeled it and walked towards where he'd seen the procession stop the previous night, chewing on the soft pulp, the fresh juices seeping directly into his bones and muscles.

Dr. Salio felt like he could walk to Bamako and back, and that's almost what he did.

"I'm gonna have to learn to position myself relative to the tree, hé!" Doctor Salio said to a woman standing on the spot where he had seen the man kneel, holding the dead baby before laying it in the roots.

He'd gone the wrong way around the tree and what should have taken ten minutes had taken almost forty, but he wasn't out of breath, in fact he was barely winded, his legs feeling stronger than ever.

The woman didn't respond. She stared at the spot between the stomach-high roots. She wore a head wrap as well, blue and green, and a green dress with yellow patches. There was no trace of the child. There was hardly any life in the woman's eyes either.

"The child was yours?" he asked.

She nodded, but didn't say anything.

"My condolences."

"Ha!" she barked. "Say that to this silly tree." She looked up at the branches, "You hear me, you hear us all, you see us all, and you take everything away!"

He moved in to comfort her.

She pushed him away. "Don't touch me! You think you know things doctor man, but you don't. Leave me alone!"

And she walked away.

———

The sun was setting by the time he walked up the small incline to the Tree Mother's hut. It hadn't taken very long to get used to the stagnating air and the bone-melting humidity of the place. Aisha was waiting for him at the entrance of the dirt path, her long black hair covering her breasts.

"Everything alright doctor?" she asked, and greeted him with a strong hug.

"Call me Salio," he said, holding her a moment longer.

"Alright, Salio come in."

Aisha took him by the hand towards the hut.

As they walked up the dirt path he noticed two of the village women stepping out of the hut, also hugging a Tree Mother as they left.

Aisha saw him look. "They come help us with some of our special needs. We cannot do everything ourselves. There is a lot of...experience in Kalakoro."

"The people here are remarkably healthy," he said as the two, tall women walked passed him, giving him a glance.

"Yes. We have lost a lot but we've been blessed in other ways."

They walked into the hut. It was empty save for a couple of village women, dusting the floor. The other Tree Mothers were in their rooms or elsewhere, the rugs and pillows lying on the floor in a circle.

"How was your day?" she asked.

He scratched his head. "It was good," he answered. "I met some people, and you were right. They've been very hospitable, but there were a couple of strange things..."

"Strange?" she asked as they walked towards her room.

"Well, yes, it's the men I've seen. They suffer from a very unique condition, and one of the villagers said they were...pregnant?"

Aisha laughed, he wanted to turn her head and kill her laughter with his lips. "Yes they are. In a matter of speaking. See, we believe that there is a spiritual connection between the mother, the father and the child, and when a woman gets pregnant, it is customary for her husband to carry the burden of pregnancy with her, and he gains weight, and she attends to him. Sometimes the bond is so strong, that the changes are very deep, but they are not pregnant, not in that sense."

Dr. Salio nodded. "Psychosomatic."

She frowned.

"It's when you believe something so much your body makes it happen."

"Yes, that's correct."

"So the C-section scars..."

"Yes!" she said, smiling, "they get them when their wife delivers, it shows that the man is a father...or was..."

"But the women don't look very pregnant, or at all."

"Women go through great lengths to hide their pregnancy,

knowing the child will likely die. They deliver before term, they never get that big."

"And the father buries the child as well?"

"Yes, that's what you saw yesterday."

They walked into her room, the last sunrays breaking through her small window. She had more furniture than he had seen in the other huts. A large bed, and an old hand crafted chair with elephant tusks as a frame, a closet and a small table with an oil lamp, two small chairs, and some torn, second hand books.

She pulled the chair and poured some tea from a small mug on the table, and began slicing some fruit.

"Look, it's probably nothing," he started, taking a sip of the cold tea. "But I stopped by where they buried the child last night. There was this woman who said the child had been hers. She was upset. Cursing at the tree, and defensive."

Aisha frowned, but seemed to dismiss it.

"Fatoumata? Yes, she has taken her loss to heart, and suffered some complications during her pregnancy. She shouldn't live much longer, she's angry about that as well. The Mother Tree is as good a scapegoat as any."

He grunted. The village was strange, but nothing that didn't make sense if you put it in context. They *did* have odd beliefs, and that was usually enough to damn you in a place where everybody else held another.

She looked out the window at the dry forest and breathed in deeply. "So what is it you wanted to talk about? You are free to stay as much as you like, you've done us a great service and the people can use your help."

"Helping is exactly what I wanted to talk about. The children, we noticed they were...different."

She nodded.

"Are all the children born this way?"

"Some, yes." she said gravely.

"Don't you want to know why?"

A tear left her eye. He hadn't expected that. She walked up to the small window. "I know why this happens. We all do. Terrible things happened in this village, horrible, horrible things…"

"Yes I know…"

"No. No you don't."

He rose and stood behind her. Her waste an inch away from his.

"We are paying for all the harm done here. That's why you never see us. Only the children are innocent. Deformed but innocent, and they are beautiful. You've seen them. Aren't they?" she implored.

He drew her into his arms. "Yes, they are."

She turned and kissed him. Catching him off guard with the intensity of her lips.

"Thank you," she repeated between kisses.

He felt aroused, harder than he had been in his life. He wanted to push her head out the window and have his way with her.

What if she too…

He went limp.

He almost pulled away but her lips demanded him. He ran his hand down her leg and up her saran. Dreading what he would find, he let his hand slip between her thighs. He felt her warm dampness, and his fingers froze unable to go further up. He let her lips draw him in, and went all the way, and found…nothing, she had only one, and it was soft and inviting.

CHAPTER 5

Dr. Salio lost himself in her hair.

It was now morning, he could hear it by the sounds of the village drifting through the window. She was his first in two years. He'd had plenty of opportunities, but his mind was on the job, and when the job was dissecting botched excisions, well, he couldn't think of things any other way.

Until last night.

And again, this morning.

The fruit had some effect on his virility. He was harder than ever, sex lasted longer. The thing was a miracle. Truly. *If the other villages knew.* But if they did they would swarm this place and probably kill the fruit before they could do anything about it.

"Good morning," she said, kissing his neck.

"Good morning," he replied, looking at the curve of her nose and wondering where she'd been all his life.

"Slept ok?"

"Better than I have in my life."

"Good," she said cuddling him.

He did feel better, unbelievably so, and for a moment forgot what he had come for in the first place, the warmth of her embrace sweeping his mind clear.

"Look. I came here because something isn't right. You all look incredibly healthy, your tree provides you all the food you need,

your water is pure, but your children are either stillborn, or...
what's your word for that?"

"Tyétémousotéw."

"Tyétémousotéw." He repeated. "I have delivered babies for
years, tended to mothers before that, run blood tests, everything.
Let me run some tests on the people here, the pregnant couples
particularly and some of the children too; no one should die of
complications on top of losing their child. I can try to understand
what is happening. I *can* understand what is happening."

She thought silently for a moment.

"I know you think you're paying for..." he started.

"I'm not thinking anything," she said quietly. "But we are in
your debt, so you can if you wish, but I do not speak for the
villagers. You are asking for something very intimate, they will
have to get to know you first, and that will take time."

"I promised my colleagues at the clinic I would be back to the
village in five days now. But I can come back, help with the sick
and wounded, they'll trust me."

She patted him on the chest. "There is something else."

"What is it?" he asked, taking another whiff of her hair.

"I'm pregnant."

He bolted upright, rolling her off of him. "What?! How?!"

"You know how."

"How do you even know?"

"I know," she said, sitting upright. "I feel it. The Tree Mothers
are very fertile."

"That's crazy! Aren't you going to wait and be sure?"

"I am sure."

This is crazy. This place is crazy.

"Look. I've studied this for years. I've practiced this for years,
hé. Some women claim to know, but they're almost always
wrong, or they already know but have a penchant for the
dramatic."

"This is not a penchant. It is day outside. You came here two
days ago. I am pregnant. Some things just are. I will let you take a
blood sample if you wish."

He breathed out and let himself fall back on the mattress.

Just what I needed. This has gotta be some kind of joke, she really...

"Aisha!" One of the other Tree Mothers called, running into their room. "Aisha, please come. Fatoumata has passed."

———————

There was blood on the floor of Fatoumata's hut, a stream of it. Her body was on a bed, her dress heavily stained at the crotch and drying with blood all around her pelvis. Her face was twisted in a rictus, either of pain, or defiance he couldn't tell. Her husband sat on a chair across from her body, his eyes red and moist.

"It was so sudden, Mother Aisha. She was fine and then after eating, suddenly she..."

He buried his face in his hands. Aisha laid a hand on his shoulder.

"It's the anger that got her Lassana," Aisha told the husband, "it ate her up, made things worse..."

Dr. Salio took a step towards the body, but Lassana launched at him. "What do you think you're doing?"

Dr. Salio raised up his hand. "It's ok. I'm an obstetric..."

"It's not ok! This is my wife!" Lassana roared.

He backed up a few steps.

"It's alright Lassana. He meant no harm," Aisha said.

Lassana collapsed back in his chair, weeping.

Aisha looked at Doctor Salio, eyes firm and shaking her head discreetly.

Well, she had told me to be careful...

He stared at the blood and the body, and a rare gust of wind blew through the window and the ground rumbled. He reached for the small table for something to hold and the floor by the door began slithering, as if a dozen snakes were sliding just beneath the surface towards the blood on the floor.

The ground stopped shaking but the shapes kept moving, meeting under the thickest patch of blood, and writhing hungrily.

The patch looked as if it was boiling, and slowly seeped into the ground in tiny suctions, until it was all gone.

The slithering shapes withdrew, and a rumble started outside.

Dr. Salio ran for the door. The mountainous trunk of the tree was contracting and expanding. The bark cracking in places and bleeding sap. Another gust of wind blew through the branches, and the trunk contracted with the creaking of old wooden floors and was silent.

———————

"What are you going to say when you get back?" Aisha asked him, standing by the hill that led out of the village and into the forest.

Nothing at all. They'll think I'm crazy.

"That everything is fine," Dr. Salio says, "and that I'll be coming back for a while longer to run some tests. Look, don't worry I won't tell them about your fruit, even if I did they'd only think this place was worse."

I won't tell them about the blood either, or that I'm gonna be a father....Looks like I'm believing it myself.

"I'll be back in a couple of weeks," Dr. Salio continued. "I can't run the tests at the clinic, but there's a lab in Sikasso." He put his hand on her stomach. "If you are right, I'll let you know."

She smiled slyly. "I am right. You'll see...The children will guide you back." She put a hand on his arm. "You're a good man Salio. Come back."

She turned away without looking back at him, joining the other Tree Mothers, and leaving without further ceremony.

"This way, doctor man," The little girl who'd almost died called from ahead of him on the path. "I must be home early this time!"

CHAPTER 6

Nurse Aissatou lifted her mug and rang it against Dr. Salio's. The small restaurant in Kolondiéba was dark, but the beer was always fresh, and after nearly two weeks, Dr. Salio needed one. He'd left a lot of work behind.

"Cheers," she said.

"Cheers," he replied, taking a deep gulp. "Are you sure the girl is gonna be alright?"

"Yeah, I left her with Stephanie, she'll be fine." She took a swig. "You know what that girl told me before we left? That she wasn't a whore. She said that twice, she was almost crying. She wasn't a whore. Even with the surgery done she would stay a virgin till she got married. She said she knew who she was, and didn't want that to be defined by what was taken from her."

"She's a strong one."

"Yes. I was thinking we could talk to U.N Women, see if we can get some funding for training and keep her around."

"Her family will come knocking soon. We have to get her to the shelter in Bamako. It's not safe for her at the village."

Nurse Aissatou frowned but nodded. "I'll keep an eye out for her. Now, you've been awfully tight lipped since you came back. You look good though. What did they feed you over there?"

He had been tight lipped. There was really no place he could start that would make sense, not without getting more questions, and he had promised not to answer this one.

"Alright, never mind me asking," Aissatou said, taking another sip.

"It's not like that. There just isn't very much to say…" All he had to go by were Aisha's vague answers. Truth was he had no idea, so he lied a little. "It's all pretty dull and dusty. There are other children that are hermaphrodites, or so they tell me. But I don't see much of them. The people are decent enough, but they don't know me, they're grateful, but I need more time."

"Ground breaking research, hé?" she teased him.

He hadn't thought about that, but it would be. He laughed. "Yes. Imagine. Dr. Salio Sanogo: from fixing clits to chicks with dicks. I would look wonderful, hé. A career move for sure."

"You're not funny."

"Good. I was going for cynical."

"Well at least you had that young woman agree to the sample, how did you do that?"

"I am not sure who she is. I can't tell if she's the chief, the others seem to defer to her… They have this council that runs the village, mostly young women. But she's the one who thanked and greeted me. They were all happy to have the kids back you should have seen them. Maybe she was assigned to me by the council, maybe not. But she said they owed me, and maybe it would encourage the others. Otherwise I tended to small cuts and sore throats."

"Well, you'll get the results in a couple of days, and you made yourself useful. You know, no one has visited them since whatever happened, happened, and you should hear the…

"Doctor!" A hand landed on his back "Thought I recognized your voice. Been a while, hé?"

It was Moctar. He looked less angry than he had the last time he'd seen him.

"I told you, your daughter would turn out ok," Dr. Salio answered him dryly.

"She did. I had some business in Bamako and Sikasso, but my wife tells me she is fine. You were right, and you've come back, you are lucky."

Uninvited, he pulled up a blue plastic chair and seated himself, digging into their small plate of peanuts. "So," Moctar started, his eyes shining. "What did you see, hé? Tell me. Are the rumors true?"

Dr. Salio and Aissatou looked at each other.

Salio had been dodging villagers for a week. He wasn't about to start with him. "What rumors?"

"You know. About how the women procreate together and have the deformed children?"

"I'm sorry. What was that? Did you say women procreating *together*?"

"Yes! They're not really women you see, and when they...get together, their children have both sexes."

Aissatou choked on her beer and spread some across the table. Dr. Salio stared at Moctar flatly.

"See what I was telling you?" she asked him, laughing.

"Women who are not women having children with women? Men with lady parts?" he shook his head. "Look Moctar, I know it is strange for you, and that you were worried for your daughter, but everything is fine now. Those children have visited before and nothing happened, right? But please, don't ask me silly questions, hé. I'm a doctor, hé, not a sorcerer."

Moctar stood up, his face dark. "You were there a week, and you didn't see anything? And you call me silly? I'm tired of trying to warn you doctor know-it-all. You wait and see."

A couple of days after the encounter with Moctar, little Amadou called from outside the clinic, "Doctor! "A letter for you! From Sikasso."

Dr. Salio barged out of the clinic, his gloves covered in blood, still wearing his facemask.

Amadou dropped the letter with a shriek and ran away.

Dr. Salio peeled off his gloves, picked up the small package, and tore it open frantically. He found he was shaking all over and his armpits were starting to tingle with nervous sweat. He wiped his brow and unfolded the results.

Certificate of Analysis- SIKASSO LABS

- **COMPOUND TESTED:** HCG 5,000 IU Vial
- **LOT NUMBER:** 16705
- **STORAGE:** 20°C to 25°C (68°F to 77°F)
- **CONTAINER:** (15) 8 mL Clear Vials

Potency Analyses   **Specification: 80 – 125%**

Analyte	Expected Amount	Unit	Results	% Expected	Test Method
Human Chorionic Gonadotropin	5000	IU	5400	109.1%	ELISA

Microbiology Report

Analysis	Results	Test Method	Pass/Fail
Sterility	Sterile	USP<71>	Pass
Endotoxin (Limit 0.03 EU/U)	0.0034 EU/U	USP<85>	Pass
Method Suitability	Verified	USP<71>	Pass

Her hCG count was through the roof. He was gonna be a father.

CHAPTER 7

"Where is Aisha?" Dr. Salio asked of the guards that met him as he approached the hill.

The markings left by the children had helped him reach the clearing, but the guards hadn't lied. Once you passed it, the baobab was all you needed to find your way, even though it disappeared sometimes it always popped up to show you the way safely to Kalakoro.

"She is resting," one of them answered.

"Is she alright?" he asked, worried. If women delivered so many stillborn and had postnatal complications, anything could happen.

"Yes, she is, but she needs her rest. The Tree Mothers take good care of each other. We will lead you."

Walking into the village, he noticed something was missing. "What happened to the other guard?" Phrasing it was still odd to him. "The pregnant one?"

The guard ahead of him answered without turning back. "His water broke. He is at home in labor, and tended to by his wife. It should be a few more hours, until we have a happy event."

Right.

The dirt path to the blue hut was lit with torches even though twilight was barely settling in, and the moon still competed with the sky for light.

He'd tried to keep her out of his mind while he was back in

Seledougou but the results had sent his blood racing, and his heart...well, he had a duty at the clinic, but he also had one to his unborn child.

And what child?

Chanting came from the hut, drifting down the path towards him, beckoning him.

The curtain of kori on the door brushed aside and a shape stood outlined against the light.

Aisha!

The guards made way for him, and he walked briskly up the path and to the door, trying hard not to run.

Her smile soothed his heart, growing bigger as he got closer. He pulled out the paper, waving it in the air.

"I've got the results! You were right, you..."

She turned sideways when he was just a few feet from her, revealing the perfect curve of her nose, the slopes of her breast, and the small two-month bulge on her stomach.

He stopped and dropped the letter.

She turned back and threw her arms around his neck, pressing her breasts against his shirt.

"I told you, you would see."

"It's only been two weeks," he said the next morning, still in shock. "In all my years as an obstetrician I have never..."

She put a finger on his lips. "I told you the Tree Mothers were very fertile. Don't worry, everything is fine. I can feel it."

What was he supposed to say? She'd been right the first time. And for the first time, he was completely out of his waters. "How long until you deliver?"

"A few weeks, at most."

"And you're sure it will be fine?"

"She will be fine. And yes. I am sure."

He was about to ask how she could be so certain about the sex of the child this early, but then again her answer would be the same.

"I heard one of the guards had gone into labor."

"Musa Kabbah? Yes. Thankfully. This pregnancy was particularly hard on him."

"I could tell. Um .., when is he due?"

"The midwife thinks it should be any moment now."

"Can I help? I'm very good at this, and maybe it will help in understanding why the baby is dead. If the baby is dead."

"The baby is dead. Make no mistake. I told you we are paying. But I'm afraid you cannot attend, they will not let you in; you're still a stranger here. Most people don't even know you are back, and don't care."

"Can I speak to his wife after she's delivered?"

"It doesn't work like that. The burden was on Musa. You'll have to talk to him directly, but not for a week or so. He needs to recover from the ordeal."

The baby was dead, and dipped in a vat of resin from the Mother Tree to keep the body from decaying while the parents got well.

Musa had lost almost all the weight in the week since he'd delivered, and now, a fresh ceremonial scar across his stomach, he held his dead infant before the tree for all to see before burying it.

"I'll talk to him before I leave tomorrow," Dr. Salio told Aisha watching the burial from a distance.

She shook her head. "They will mourn now. You may try if you wish."

"I'm tired of watching this. It's pointless. The same thing happens every time. What are you hoping for, that the tree will save you somehow? Is that what you're gonna do to our daughter?"

"Our daughter is to become a Tree Mother."

"And never leave the village?"

"It's more complicated than that. Let's go back to the hut."

Dr. Salio tossed under the light sheets with Aisha next to him, impervious to his nightmare-filled groans, cold sweat running down his neck and onto his chest, staining the mattress.

His daughter appeared and disappeared in his sleep. He saw the tree's root slither into her bedroom and drag her across the floor screaming, then through the village and squeezing her under the tree in a spurt of blood.

The screams turned to breathless moans and then to orgasm somewhere inside the hut. He woke up fully erect with the image of his dead daughter seared across his eyes.

The moaning didn't stop, and didn't wake Aisha.

He walked out of bed. He couldn't release into Aisha with the bloody child on his mind, so he went towards the direction of the moaning, and found the door locked, walked out of the hut and around it towards the small windows of the Tree Mothers' rooms.

The full moon shone directly behind the hut, lending wavy shadows to the blue pigments used to cover the walls.

The moans were clearer here. The windows let them bounce a little on the air, and then lose themselves in the immensity. Such a small, but revealing thing.

He kept his back to the wall as he crept towards the window where the moaning came from. He had no idea why he was here, it was none of his business, but in three weeks altogether in Kalakoro, he hadn't gotten a single answer. He would have this one.

He leaned into the opening, careful not to let the moon cast a shadow, and caught two Tree Mothers in a sixty-nine, the woman nearest to the foot of the bed, her hands grasping the other's buttocks firmly, while her wrapped head buried itself between willowy brown legs, her own, round rump riding the other's...*wait, the Tree Mothers never wrap their hair...that's a woman from the village.* He grinned. *Special needs, hé? Moctar would have a field day.*

A pair of hands closed on his mouth and eyes, and dragged him back, quickly and firmly. He kept his mouth shut. The grip was too soft to be one of the guards, and the last thing he wanted...

"Aisha?" He whispered when he turned as the hands uncovered his eyes and ears.

She winked at him, naked in the moonlight, their daughter easily at four months protruding to cover half the moon.

"This is not for you," she said, smiling seductively, and took him by the hand as the moaning intensified.

"How much longer are you gonna be?" Dr. Salio asked Aisha, his hand on her stomach, the nine other Tree Mothers waiting behind them on the path by the hill. It had felt dismissive the first time, but the second time gave it an air of solemnity.

"Not very long," she said absently, staring into his eyes. "This is going very well. There will be another Tree Mother soon."

"You never told me what you meant by that."

She turned to the others, who nodded as if understanding the question, or perhaps she had just discussed it with them when he wasn't around. He wondered which of the women it was he'd caught the night before. He couldn't tell. *Gazelles, to the last one of them.* If his own daughter looked like that he would have to keep an eye out for her.

She turned back to him. "The Tree Mothers are here to teach. In the same way the Mother Tree protects us. We have learned something from the children. We can't let them come this close to getting killed again. We cannot be scared and punish ourselves for what was done here. Not anymore. The next Tree Mother will go out into the world, and teach them as well. People have much to learn."

CHAPTER 8

Dr. Salio felt no peace when we went back to Seledougou. He couldn't sleep. Every thought consumed by Aisha and his child. He couldn't eat either. Accras were too greasy. But then steaks were too fatty, and mangoes too juicy.

There was too much of everything in everything except in that fruit.

"Are you sure you aren't hungry?" Aissatou asked sitting in the small patio behind the clinic. "You have hardly eaten in days."

"Yeah, must have caught something over there. Feel fine though. Think of it as a cut on the budget."

"We don't need cuts on the budget, your little CNN stunt funded us for three years, all continental donations too, hé. People love you doc."

"Yeah but we're swarming with journalists. I'm glad I'm leaving again tomorrow."

———

Moctar was on the square trying to hold on to an Australian reporter Dr. Salio had agreed to meet the day before.

The man looked like he didn't know whether to punch Moctar in the face or draw away politely as he was. His right arm was twitching.

Moctar let go and the reporter approached Dr. Salio. "G'day there mate! That fella sure is a dag, makes a big note of himself. Wanted an interview, front page he said."

He sat down and pulled out a cigarette.

"Oh yeah, Moctar sure is something. What's he on about now, John?" Dr. Salio asked.

The Australian whistled, drew a puff and shook his head. "Crazy story mate, crazy story...Said something about a village easts of here, in the shade of a giant tree. Did a lot of cutting over there. Your mate says it's as big as mountains, thousands years old. Heard some stuff like that before in the Outback, in the Dreamtime. Anyway, he says, it's not a tree at all, but an old spirit, and it got angry at all the cutting. I sure would. He says that, well, one day they were up to cut this Sheila, real spunk the girl, and they did the bloody bastards, but they accidentally dropped her skin, and the roots of the tree came out of the ground and gobbled the clitoris off the floor, and slid back down."

"What?!" Aissatou yelled. Dr. Salio swallowed his saliva. He thought of Aisha and felt sick, but the thought of the tree made him hungry.

"Fair dinkum mate. But that's not all he said. Apparently there was a drought yes? They couldn't get a thing to grow and just when they were starving the tree started growing fruit, and starving as they were they gobbled it up."

So did I. I can't get enough of it.

"After a few weeks." John continued "The girls who'd been cut, started growing their clitorises back, poetic justice I guess, but the men and, the older women who'd did the cutting...they changed he says. The men lost their willies and the women grew willies, and since all they have are stillborn and hermaphrodites."

And Salio trailed off and knew he had to get back to Aisha and tell her what the Australian told him...

"And that's the story as he told it." Dr. Salio finished telling Aisha.

Her stomach was passed the six month mark; it wouldn't be more than a few days.

"Now," he went on, "that's insane, even by standards here, but how would he know exactly how the tree reacted, hé? You never explained that one either by the way. I want to help, I really do, but I've been here and back for a month now, I have work at the clinic, no one here will let me talk to them anyway..."

He wanted to say he might as well leave, but his daughter chose that moment to kick, and Aisha's stomach rippled with it.

"See how strong she is?" she asked looking at her stomach.

"You're coming to term in barely a few days. Who are you? You're the girl from the story aren't you?"

"So you believe the story?"

Do I?

"No! Of course not!"

"The girl from the story is my sister. She died."

"I'm sor..."

"And yes, that's why we have so little water. The Mother Tree drinks everything you drop, she laps the blood off the floor, it has always been this way, she is an old tree, she has lasted longer than our civilizations, she has her own ways. But what was done here. All the girls... Yes, there is a curse here, but we will open up, our daughter..."

"How did your sister die?" he asked.

"We were supposed to be excised together one night. We were woken up in the middle of the night, with beating drums and the older women clapping and chanting. Then they brought us to the roots of the Mother Tree. We'd heard things of course, but the girls who were cut and complained were quickly silenced or marked as crazy...I was lucky my sister went first. I wasn't allowed to watch but I heard her ask what was happening, her voice trembling asking what the knife was for and then her screams. The blood usually stops before they sew you up, but it didn't stop for my sister. The blood kept pouring and the tree kept drinking, and she died. I was lucky. My mother had second thoughts after that. A few weeks later, the drought started..."

No one even bothered to find out what went wrong...

He laid his head on her stomach, listening for his daughter's heartbeats. No matter what, she wouldn't have to go through this. "They cut the clitoral artery, her blood didn't clot properly and she died from protracted bleeding," he said, remembering his older sister's own screams, while he'd laid in bed shaking. *Perhaps we do share something after all.*

He'd never seen her again. He'd turned his back on his family, his country and his culture because of this.

And here he was and kissed her on the stomach. "Get some rest now. And have some fruit. You're almost due."

CHAPTER 9

Dr. Salio walked under the shade of the tree and routinely picked up one of the fruit lying around, unpeeled it and took a bite.

It was good to taste it again, he felt the nutrients flood his system and the juices fill his pallet. He had gained weight on the steady diet of fruit, and all of it muscle, as if every single effort, anything as simple as walking was a full lower body workout.

He looked up at the branches, covered in hundreds of hundreds of fruit. There might have been more, higher up in the branches, but if they ever hit the ground they'd be mush, and it was dark up there, looking into the branches was like staring into space.

He finished the first fruit and picked up another one, and peeled it off.

Now just imagine, just a second, that that crazy story is true.

The shape was odd, he'd thought of a mushroom and a banana. That was true, but a cruder person would have said he was biting into a dick.

It did have a similar shape, an elongated shaft, and a thicker mushroom cap head. The way it split at the bottom jogged something in his memory.

It split into two strands, as if to wrap around something. That was very distinct.

I should know this... it's shaped like a penis, and has longer tissue to wrap around a larger area, just like a cli...

He fell back, crawling away from the tree and through the ripe clitorises...*fruit*, he thought firmly, *ripe fruit. They're fruit. It's just a shape. It's a just a coincidence. It's an amazing fruit, can't it have a strange shape? That doesn't prove anything. Someone had to chew through a pineapple to find out it was good. Anything can happen, hé...*

But anything couldn't happen. Certainly not everything that happened in Kalakoro, *and she always has an answer for everything, a very simple answer, but it doesn't add up.*

He heard grunts from a nearby hut. Grunts and moans. He'd heard those before but up until he'd peeped on the Tree Mother, he hadn't wanted to invade anybody's privacy, but at this point...

He leaned into the window. It faced the tree and the view outwards was dark, and the groans intensified.

A couple was naked on their bed, in the missionary position. From the window he stared at the husband's back, thrusting angrily into his wife who groaned with every thrust.

He followed the wife's muscular legs, up to surprisingly hairy calves, and caught a glimpse of the husband's bright head wrap...

He managed to crawl back between the roots of the tree before hurling.

A head wrap...she's between her *husband's* legs. *She's thrusting...into* her *husband!*

They're not really women you see, they have wulus, and the men have lady parts, it's the fruit you see... He heard Moctar say.

His water broke. He is at home in labor... He heard the guard say.

See, we believe that there is a spiritual connection between the mother, the father and the child...

He grabbed for his genitals, found them there and flaccid, wretched again, and the groaning stopped.

They caught me. They're gonna feed me to this thing, shove me into the roots like they do the babies...

"Everything ok Doctor Salio?" he heard the wife's voice call at him.

She hasn't seen me...

He wiped his lips. "Yes! I'm fine. Don't know what happened, must have caught something back home."

"Ha! You gotta be careful with outside food. The Mother Tree is good to us!"

Yes, yes it is, he thought, nodding at her and walking back to the Tree Mother's hut.

When he arrived at the small entrance to the dirt path, one of them brushed passed him. He didn't know her name but now he knew which one he'd caught in bed with one of the village women that night. She smiled at him as she walked passed, rubbing a two-month bulge on her stomach.

Aisha ran down the path towards him, and almost toppled him with the strength of her embrace.

"I'm almost there, Salio! Two more days and you will be a father. Isn't it wonderful?"

Dr. Salio wasn't allowed to attend the delivery, but waited outside the hut, anxious for that first wail. *It's not coming, and if it comes what is it gonna be?*

He waited in the stale and humid night air, in the glow of the guards' torchlight, a crowd of villagers behind him, equally silent, equally anticipating.

A thin screech broke through clogged lungs and through the hut's walls. The oxygen pushed the fluid from the lungs into the blood, and the screeched deepened, turning into a wail that echoed painfully inside the hut and through the windows and into the village.

The tree rumbled behind them.

The kori were pushed open and a Tree Mother stepped out, waving him in.

Dr. Salio rushed in. Aisha was on the floor in the center, lying on piled up rugs, with pillows supporting her back. The Tree Mothers stood around her and she was attended by one of the village women. She held a small shape wrapped in a blanket in her arms.

He shoved his way through the Tree Mothers, and looked at Aisha.

She looked exhausted. Her eyes were heavy and she was glistening with sweat, but the child breathed under the blanket. *She* breathed.

"Do you want to hold her?" she asked.

He took the baby from her arm and opened the blanket before he could think.

She was a little girl. A simple little girl.

The tree rumbled again.

"The Mother Tree wants us to present her the child. We must not let her wait."

The Tree Mothers showed him to the doors, helping Aisha rise and follow behind him.

They're letting me keep the baby...

He passed the threshold, and the villagers let him through, along with Aisha and the Tree Mothers; bowing their heads as he walked by.

The tree creaked and rumbled rhythmically. A creak and a rumble, inhaling and exhaling. The roots, that infiltrated all of the village's grounds shook along with it, buoying his walk with little wavelets of earth, and behind the procession the drum roll picked up, but not the mournful slog of a burial, it was upbeat, and eager.

Bam – Bambadambam-bambam

Bambadambam, Bam

Bambadambam – Bambam...

Maybe she isn't lying this time.

But he couldn't take the risk, he had to seize the first chance he'd get.

The tree came into full view around the small bend.

The thick grey-brown trunk oozed sap and resin, the bark fissured like leaking wounds, its man-sized roots twitching like spider legs knitting a web, and the branches bellowed, the sound caught inside the maze, ricocheting with a cackle.

The path bifurcated ahead of him. To the left it led towards the tree, to the right to the small hill and into the forest away from Kalakoro.

I'll only have a second. And how fast can I run?

He wrapped the blanket tighter. The drumroll gained speed as they approached the tree that seemed to grow more excited at each of their steps. He picked up his pace, just a little, enough to gain a couple of yards. That's all he would get. He reached the bifurcation, held his little girl close to his chest and ran.

The drumming stopped. Two spears landed ahead and next to him.

"Don't kill my daughter!" he heard Aisha scream behind him.

The tree roared. Branches the size of smaller trees writhed and cracked brontide against each other like thunder.

The roots tried to stop him, but they didn't seem determined. The ground rose and fell hard. It was all he could do not to drop the tiny, crying bundle in his arms, but he held on, because the roots wouldn't harm the child either.

The guards were almost on him, and he was almost to the hill.

What was I thinking? That I would outrun Hussein Bolt through his forest?

The tree was making it easy for the guards. They didn't have to sprint over an earthquake.

I'm not even gonna make it to the tree line, he thought as he turned the bend around the hill and out of Kalakoro. He couldn't look behind. *They're gonna catch me any second now,* he thought, feeling their hands already creeping on his shoulders, their arms around his legs throwing him down, and the shaking ground stopped.

Dr. Salio stumbled forward but held on for the baby's sake, lest he crushed her in his fall.

He turned around.

The villagers, the guards and the Tree Mothers were standing at the bend, at the very edge of the hill, and didn't move further.

"Thank you for taking me out into the world," a knowing voice said rising from his chest.

He looked down and saw his baby girl wink at him.

He dropped the child.

The villagers gasped as Dr. Salio scrambled to catch her, but she hit the ground without a sound.

"No!" he screamed, but the blanket shook, and a six-month-old baby crawled out from under it. By the time it got to its knees it was six, by time it stood to his waste it was twelve, and before he could say a word, a beautiful young woman, the spitting image of her mother, stood naked before him.

He couldn't move. He couldn't speak, and staring into her eyes he knew something was missing. The grey of her pupil never ended, it swirled forever backwards like a whirlpool. She was hollow, inside her eyes an echo harkened back into an infinity of darkness.

"Father," she said, breaking the silence.

"What are you?" That wasn't his daughter no matter what she called him. That was not a person, there was none of him in there.

She looked surprised, and turned her head towards the quiet tree, her eyes leaking sticky, translucent sap.

"I am the tree."

The next Tree Mother will go out into the world...

Aisha stood behind the bend looking at him, a calm smile on her lips, all the passion he had seen in her eyes gone.

She hadn't lied, the one thing she didn't lie about.

"They cannot leave the village grounds, but I can now, thanks to you."

...People have much to learn...

"But the children..."

"The children can leave, until they can no longer eat outside food that is. My fruit is good isn't it?"

His hand shot for his crotch, he couldn't find the lumps; he reached around and couldn't find the shaft.

"The transformation takes a few weeks. Yours should be complete by now."

He reached into his jeans, there was the pubic hair, and then his fingers reached the moist patch between his legs, the thick lips, and rubbed against his tiny, tiny clitoris.

He felt wetter. He felt dead. He felt his mouth water.

He reached for her throat, but his weak arms couldn't reach her. She dodged him easily, and tripped him, Dr. Salio falling helplessly on his back.

"You can never leave either," she said, as the children came running out of the path, laughing and pushing each other.

They grabbed him by the arms, three at a time.

"Come Doctor Salio!"

"Yes doctor! Come we'll have fun!"

"Yes! And we'll have fruit!"

They began to pull. Dr. Salio found he couldn't resist. His strength was gone, but more than that, he wanted to be back in the village, and have fruit, and...

"But you will have babies for me, father. You will lay them in the roots and lend me their strength," she turned, her silhouette drawn against the moonlight and took a step further away. "I have to go now; there is much for me to do in the world."

She took another step, and the children drew Salio behind the hill.

THE WHORES,
THE DEALER,
&
THE DIAMOND

The most beautiful things are found in the darkest holes...

THE WHORES

Whores aren't bad people, but these two were, or perhaps they were just bitter and jealous, which in many ways is the same thing, but these two conspired. Conspired against the beautiful diamond in their midst, probably because she reminded them of how far they'd come, or how short a way in such a long time, the skin on their faces drawn like the parchment of the map that led to them.

One was still young, and pretty by local standards, plus or minus a few years hooking. It didn't help she was a compulsive liar and occasionally dabbled in fencidil around the candle-lit chop and cha stands of Bangla Bazar or the slums along the railroad tracks.

Their hole of a home was too small for her. Dug in a depression on the side of the road, there wasn't much height to it, and it flooded easily. At least on the job she was out all night and didn't have to be reminded of how low she had to stoop, or lay her eyes on the glowing gem, seeming to draw all the light and energy out of the air, the dingy room, and even herself.

She was still pretty and thin enough not to waste hours fixing her make up between passes, but she also had more work. Small men with little prospects, with, ironically, the decency to pay instead of raping her.

It could have been worse. She had all her teeth and her own hair, light grey eyes and no scars on her face yet. Other girls worked there too, their skin melted in folds over their face where bits of teeth showed through holes in their cheeks. Some men still wanted them; it must have helped them a little, knowing they could still be desired, even if for a fleeting moment of acid fetish in the humid dark of threadbare sheets. She had only gotten a beating when they'd found she wasn't a virgin and the thirty-five year old man she'd been set to marry set off to find himself another twelve-year-old.

She had grown into it, it was the family trade after all, but for some reason the golden lily reading in her chair was immune. Not that dozens of men didn't beg for her hand or for much less romantic things, but they could not have the little Diamond, so they turned to her instead, angrily and frustrated, and the little love she had for that precious, precious thing, was slowly fucked out of her.

The older one hadn't been young for a long time, and the little height didn't bother her either. The ceiling had, over the years, molded the shape of her back into an exact reflection of its curves, and everywhere she walked she bore its invisible weight as a testimony to her years, that, all things considered, were still few.

But while she didn't mind the slant that had become her life, it forced her face near the little rainbow smiling in the dark hole. It blinded what was left of her eyes, scrapped by years of dust, swept hunched over and all the foreign, filthy sweat falling from hairy chests onto her eyes at night, stinging her repeatedly until she couldn't see the beauty before her anymore.

Now, what you see is what you get, but you don't see the sausage being made very often, and with good reason. So, although the hunched over, glaring, and certainly moustached old lady in front of you, does in her current form, deserve all the judgement you may hold, she is like most of us an uneven mix of love and pain, having tilted heavily towards the latter.

There was a little girl who had been told that she ought to leave the cluster of trees by the rivulet where her father had built their nine-foot mud hut between rainy seasons. She had wondered why. Why her, and not any of her six other sisters, who were older and better prepared for the world than she was. The tallest thing she'd ever seen was the masjid in Birampur, and even then, from a distance.

They hadn't bothered to dry her tears, they hadn't turned to wave goodbye, they'd just shoved her in the car with the strange man with the greasy hair, and left.

She met other girls that night, some pretty, some not. They had fed her and bathed her and taken her to the bazar for several sharis, churis, and Chinese food and she saw more lights than she knew existed, and she had slept better than she had in her life, and woke up to find the man stroking something fleshy and smelly over her face.

The details of murder are always the same depending on the weapon, and eventually she found this man, with a hole in the ground, but enough drugs to keep the pain away, but not enough to keep her off the streets and out of other men's beds.

The Diamond was theirs. They could not know for sure, but that's who they'd wanted her to be, and she had been so proud when its light had illuminated the midwife's face. She had been standing taller back then, perhaps more air had filled her lungs and more love had filled her heart, before she knew life at the level of a rickshaw's wheels. Maybe she had been rotten all along but people seldom are. Yet what you have now is the hag, leering over what should be most precious to her.

THE DEALER

Pan and fencidil combined have the same effect on someone's mouth as a siege has on a medieval castle.

There are holes in the wall and blood running down its sides. There are bits of flesh rotting in cavities that no brush can reach, bits of chanachur poking out of sore gums like bone fragments. And when people are high they tend to smile a lot, entirely too much for comfort.

Adages about consumption and supply seldom apply, and while his business was good by Dinajpur street standards, it could have done more for his hole in the ground if he hadn't sniffed so much of it himself. Perhaps he could have afforded to dig another.

The hole had grown around him. It had started small, barely a slit between a temple wall and the concrete. It is never easy running from home, but running was better than lashes, and the fingering, and the little hole was as good a place to hide as any, if not for sewage and the occasional stray dogs looking for a place to hide and something to bite.

Dogs were an education he'd found and an easy target for motor vehicles. He would take one in at a time and fix it. If it could limp, it would limp and bite for him.

Running errands for the local mastan kept him out of the hands of bigger boys and sleazy men with finer words than their clothes accounted for. Rickshawallas stopped urinating on him from the road, and the few taka he was allowed to keep bought him a small gas light and a table by his mattress and a pound of marijuana, and the hole got bigger, and his reputation and his ego, and his habit.

As the quality of his product decreased so did his health and his loneliness, in spite of the constant buzz and laughter of the other fiends floating in the floodwater of his once glorious hole.

And one day she had fallen in. Exhausted, her lips, tongue, and teeth drenched in blood, her eyes like the monsoon winds and her face the determination of a tiger. He had taken her in, and had never asked. It was good to have someone to get high with.

He didn't beat her as much as his friends' beat their wives. And sometimes, in obscene bouts of fencidil, Carews gin, and fucking, she would grow taller and blue, filling the room with her four arms, holding his decapitated head in one of her hands, and would pull her tongue at him.

"Chamunda," he would whisper.

"Yes," she would say; ten feet tall and leering. "Yes. Worship your goddess."

Their first union had birthed another whore. He expected a junkie their second time, but unexpectedly, they had a diamond.

The Diamond smiled at him from her small mattress, her nose in her books, her eyes twinkling even in the half-light.

His wife and daughter were after her. Every day he saw it growing in their eyes. The envy, the self-loathing, the pain. But he would keep her close. Because he knew her secret. Even if she didn't.

THE DIAMOND

She cried when it rained sometimes. When she thought no one was looking, when she was tired of smiling, tired of trying to channel the pain floating inside her hole in the ground like the stench of stagnant flood water.

She hoped her tears would fade in the deluge and that they would go back into the world, seep into the ground and grow into beautiful things, beautiful thoughts to tickle and soothe people when the pain stunk too hard.

She often saw her father trailing behind when she thought she was alone. At first she'd thought he was out on his rounds, or simply lost in the haze of that thing he sniffed, but he was always there, keeping an eye on her, while her tears hit the floor and blossomed.

Her tears shone. They shone with a quality brighter than light, they glowed among the raindrops and as they poured down her cheeks, forming into tiny puddles of blue starlight at her feet.

She was skinny. So skinny, but even pulled tight over her perfect bones, her skin was toffee, and the bones that protruded in her cheeks and nose held the immortal flow of beauty, and her light brown eyes full of dreamy tears and fake smiles kept the wolves at bay.

She walked on twigs, and when she was lucky, even tiny plastic sandals, and her grey dress had been patched until it was an entirely new dress made of older dresses.

She ran around the temple grounds. If they didn't build the temple quickly someone would snatch up the spare space to build another bazar across from the bazar. She watered the plants every day, she was weak but she helped carry little stones, and if it rained, her tears would seal the mortar quicker, they would make the stones unbreakable and stick to the ground so that no man or demon could tear them away.

And every night when the sun set beneath the buildings she

would let her eyes brighten and her lips twist upward into a smile and make her way home.

Sometimes she would see her father, collecting her tears in a cup, out of a small shiny puddle on the side of the road. She would tip toe so he wouldn't see her, hoping her wish was true, and that her tears would bring a happier home.

She would be the first every morning at Sharedeshwari Girls High School in Kalitola. Before the teachers but after the pion, who had known her father in his glory days but never told her, and she would help him sweep, or teach the old man small words until the yard filled with daughters of rickshaw and chai wallas in their green and white school dresses and braided hair.

She didn't understand everything the Peace Corps volunteer tried to teach her, but she could pronounce it perfectly, be it *trees* or *Louisville slugger*. She had a golden tongue that could wrap itself around all the languages in the world, and she sat up on the front row, and passed down the answers to the other girls when the teacher wasn't looking.

She ate tiffin like it was her last meal, aloo chop and mishti, dipping the warm spicy potato cake in the sweet sugar dripping over the dessert, and since the teacher liked her sometimes she'd have two.

Sometimes her teacher would help out at the temple, and he'd help her practice her reading before he spent the night drinking adulterated vodka and playing mangir betha with the older men. She would listen to dhoom machale and mein deewana, from car radios finding their way everywhere, and think of motorcycles over rice fields, and the colorful dresses of the countryside, the raging cities she couldn't find on a map, and she would smile. Truly smile.

THE WHORES

The Whores had never learned to read. That is not a universal trait, but in this instance, circumstances couldn't have led elsewhere.

Yet illiteracy frees the mind in ways the civically educated person is unaware, and consequently often falls prey to.

Thus reading was of very little consequence to them, but it didn't help the little Diamond, her nose in a book, mistaking her smile for her lording over them the little their father and husband had to spare while they prepared for another night of sweating in the dark.

"There's a stain on your shari," the older woman told her older daughter who looked down silently and splashed a little water on the stain before it dried. She felt another sticking the dress to her buttocks, and wiggled it free without telling her mother. It was hard to tell her anything. How much she hated her for never having wanted more for her daughter, but she knew she kept her close out of love, and how often those things conflicted.

Gods appear in deserts the way conniving plots are devised under street lamps. It isn't the lamp or the street, the god or the desert, or even the person that leads to the plot. It's the voices whispering in the dark building behind, between the closed shops, where you've left something of yourself and thus try to take it from someone else.

A few rickshawallah hadn't caught customers off the last Hanif coach, and would be making their way over soon after finishing their rice wine. The halo from the lamp stretched barely across the street, their voice a barrier of sorts but only until they broke it.

There was something off; both of them knew it.

The Dealer was really an addict, although he prided himself otherwise, and he had found a new addiction in their Diamond. He had also beaten them with a branch the only time they had followed him on a rainy afternoon where she'd gone on her walks.

The oddest was how he'd disappear for hours after she'd come home, wandering in in a daze, his face shinning, his eyes holding nothing for nothing in the world except his little Diamond.

The voices beyond the light stopped their carousing, and the grinding of old wheels made its way across the street. They would walk right passed her and go for her daughter one at a time. It was hard looking at the younger version of herself, or how she could have been, hating herself for not being able to give her more, but loving her too much to let her leave.

"What do you think he's hiding?" her daughter asked.

The wallas parked their rickshaws a few feet from them under the lamp, the paintings on their carts paradoxical homages to the goddesses they were about to defile.

"He'll come for The Diamond. We have to plan this carefully, and draw him out…"

She looked at the red, vacant eyes of the four men lurching towards them. Their lips red with pan, their lungi caked with dust and sweat, and she remembered being a young girl, too young to understand what the flush of alcohol mixed with the swagger of hopelessness would mean to her, and what started off as regret bloomed into a plot, and she leaned over into her daughter's ear and shared it.

THE DEALER

He waited until she tiptoed behind him, thinking her footsteps in the puddles didn't betray her, as he gathered the shiny tears out of the puddle where they floated, darting about aimlessly with the gusts of wind like silverfish.

Love is a fleeting thing, and he knew by the smiles she had for him when she thought he wasn't looking that she took his vigilance for love. He had thought so too, when the old man had started giving him sweets as a child, then watched over him in the rice fields, then followed him in the forest in the darkness. But it wasn't love. And neither was this.

He had in a way convinced himself that it was, as one would have to, as we all do daily, but he loved her like young girls love the balloon they're holding, the way he loved all things. As long as the buzz went on. He'd never wondered if he could love anything without the buzz. The buzz was good. It kept the memories away.

The tears swarmed, even though the cup kept the wind off the water. They would meet and break, turning in concentric circles along the edges, then dashing for the middle to reunite and break again.

The curtain of rain was a blessing, if you didn't know what to listen for a whole army could march right passed you and you wouldn't know until you stabbed yourself on their spears. It was easier on nights when his wife and daughter were out. They had ears like wolves and noses just the same, and they would sniff him out given the opportunity. The Diamond fell asleep quick. All he had to do was wait a few minutes for her to drop on her mattress all cried out, and the way was clear.

The temple hid another hole, one that had been patched in with bricks long ago, but he had loosened those bricks equally long ago. Most cities are built on holes, most flooded over the years, others turned into subway tunnels, the vacuity held together by the sheer strength of will of the city itself. If those who walked its stones knew, they'd be scared to step on the pavement.

This hole ran deep beneath the foundations of the temple and bridged out, a path winding down into the unknown. He had started down that path once as a boy, until the darkness was so thick that the candle revealed nothing beyond his feet. That hole, little did anyone know, led to the edges of the plate, an ancient fault line that had long since lain dormant. He'd felt a shiver on his shoulder and ran back up, never walking down again.

He hunched over and crawled in, turning to put the bricks back behind him, the tears in the cup glowing like a weak torchlight, but enough for him to crawl further down the hole, towards a deep blue glow, lacing the old wrinkly walls in little waterfalls spreading along the cracks like raindrops through a sieve.

He emerged on the other side, his back and legs disappearing behind him into the blue glow that bathed his used face, and momentarily healed the sores inside his mouth and bleeding gums as he smiled, turned the red of his eyes the white of their youth, reflecting a hundred tiny spikes of light.

THE DIAMOND

She was playing badminton on the temple grounds when it started to rain. She had gotten there last and ended up with the only adult sized racket. It was taller than she was, and chasing the shuttlecock around felt like trying to catch a butterfly with a net, with the same elusiveness and abandon. She had managed to catch one once. It had died the next day, but the bush had held exactly the same butterfly, that same afternoon. It couldn't have been the same she'd known it, but there was something immortal about it that made her feel connected to everything, and she'd stopped chasing them.

She hit the others as often as she hit the birdie, which was more often; but when the wind rose and the raindrops started, the static on the air fueled the fun, and winning or losing mattered less than slipping in the rain and sliding in the mud.

She often wondered if the other girls cried as often as she or forced a smile as she did. They didn't need to now, they didn't think of what their mothers would do to them for what they'd done to their dresses, they'd forgotten they had homework, and probably some chores too, but what difference did a day make? They were truly happy right then, and how often did that happen?

And yet the tiny moments couldn't keep back the tears. She caught a glimpse of her father behind a tree, staying quietly at bay, and it was crusty and muddy with the dirt of childhood that she slipped into the hole.

Her mother and sisters had pulled some tarpaulin over the clay stove and the smoke built up against the low ceiling of the hole, pulling it even lower with swirling, stormy clouds with an affinity for biting little girls' eyes and hiding in their wet hair.

It was too smoky inside to read and too wet outside, but she would have to sit under the tarpaulin with them anyway. She dreaded the moments alone with them, when she had to try extra hard to keep her spirits up against the tendrils of their envy trying to seep in through her ears and nose.

In those moments she would slip back to the school trip they had taken to the Tetulia tea gardens along the northern border with India. The wispy trees and lush bushes, and the border guard had waved her over and held her over the border, floating like an *Apsara*. Where you could feel the Himalayas, hundreds of kilometers in the distance, a distortion on the horizon as far and high as the eye can see, an invisible curtain, a shimmer undulating on the air. She'd known the energy of the mountains then.

She had asked the teacher if Tetulia was where Hanuman had dropped the Dronagiri mountaintop, but her teacher didn't know and to cover it up had called her *bandur mey* for monkey girl, but luckily it hadn't stuck.

Her mother and sister were smiling tonight. Perhaps the rain would keep them off the streets. They were always nicer in those moments. The rain brought tears and laughter unevenly to her hole, but tonight it was good.

They barely glanced at her muddy dress and hair, offered her chop and chai and asked her about her day.

It's hard to forget what you haven't really known, or perhaps the fleeting moments scare you more, even the pleasant ones, and when they come to life again you forget all else. Or perhaps The Diamond was still young, and hadn't passed from a wedding ring to a pawn shop. Perhaps she was the only pure diamond left in the world, and couldn't understand the deviousness lurking behind the smiles of eyes that never truly shone with mirth.

Her sister smiled at her mother who nodded and turned to The Diamond. "The rain hurts my joints, little gem, would you mind getting me some pomade from the *dokan*?"

She looked beyond the tarpaulin, expecting tears to swell but felt none. There was a warmth inside her that evaporated them as soon as they soaked her heart.

She uncoiled from her squat and bounced up, the inkling of joy running down her veins to her skinny legs, a golden skinned Nataraj, and in that moment her hair crowned with static in a perfect halo around her head, catching a streak of lightning through a distant window in a purple glow. Even The Whores caught their breath, which is uncommon for people who had seen so much.

"Ji amu! Jachi!" The Diamond said.

The older women smiled at each other but there was something less than assured in their grin. No one wanted the gods to look too deeply into their hearts, if gods were into such things, but they didn't care for what the gods saw. They weren't sure of what they'd seen.

"Dhonnobad meyer amar," Her mother said in mock affection, ruffling her daughter's hair. "This is where to go…"

THE WHORES

Looking at The Diamond's infant mirth, her sister wondered if she had been so gullible once, concluding cynically that she wouldn't have ended where she was now had she not been. She wondered what that mirth could become, given all she hadn't had to grow and tear the world with love.

The purple halo of The Diamond's hair was still burning against her retina. It followed wherever she looked and some doubt lingered, quickly brushed off by The Diamond's joy cutting into her shredded heart.

When had she last laughed like this when she wasn't inebriated, or in the rare moments when she forgot herself enough to feel anything? She hung on to any of those things be they mirth or heartache. For a second only she remembered there was someone under all the muck and humiliation, that the child who hadn't known anything but warmth, that came out screaming one day out of an old whore's womb was still there, somewhere under the layers.

This wasn't one of those moments. She wasn't sure what it was, but she had heard the footsteps The Dealer thought he hid so well, clapping in the puddles across the street, and had smiled at her mother as they'd agreed.

She looked away as The Diamond hugged her at the knees, her little face pressed into her thighs, and stepped out into the rain a few seconds after her, anxious to catch the footsteps before they got away, nervous that in her haste he might hear her.

He did not.

She didn't walk very long. The rain caked her hair to her *orna* in an instant, the few wisps sticking through blowing with the gusts, tickling her nose. She tried hard not to sneeze. The Dealer was a cautious person and her back still bore small scars from the thrashing last they'd followed, thin pale streaks that cut through the golden she shared with The Diamond. A little bile rose in her stomach, it hadn't been the lashes that had hurt, but the fact of them.

The Dealer was kneeling on the far east corner of the temple, his form delineated through the filaments of rain, his head darting left and right in the paranoia that marked the fiend. He removed a few lose stones from the foundation wall, a light blue glow, rising from his hands illuminating his thousand year old youth's face, as he began to crawl inside.

A scream rang nearby. The scream of someone who had never faced terror before, shrill, desperate but with the slightest hint of a melody, the melody that was innocence lost.

The Diamond's screams.

She had expected them.

The Dealer had not.

He crawled backwards in a frenzy, a grunt breaking his lips as his head banged against the roof of the hole, and he darted towards the scream without replacing the stones.

She would only have a few minutes. She knew not to let her sense of time fool her, she had learned just how long a moment can feel while being abused, and how short it was when she would finally get a chance to breathe.

She lowered herself to the ground, her shawar kamiz impeding her crawl, but she went further down into the darkness, until the darkness gave way to a bluish glow, and into a small cave, little ridges carved from the floor to its ceiling along the walls, lined with thousands of tiny blue diamonds, and in a cup on the floor, dashing streaks of light suddenly froze and crystallized, and she knew The Dealer's secret, and just as a breeze forbears a hurricane, she also knew The Diamond's.

THE DEALER

He put the cup down and knelt by the temple, the tiny rips in his gums slowly stitched together by the tears glowing on his face. "Om Tare, Toutare Toure Soha; Om Tare, Toutare, Toure Soha; Om Tare..."

Mayasura, the demon king, had raised the nymph Mandodari. Hidimbi the demoness had birthed Ghatotkacha the hero, then why wouldn't a dealer and a whore bring forth a diamond?

The mantra alleviated some of the guilt. He found it worked better than fenci, but then looking into the cup and the silverfish tears gracing the rain, he found himself plunged into a deep trance, sometimes barely conscious of his surroundings, but that had been the default position of his consciousness for as long as he could remember, and he knew to navigate it well.

No matter how many drops fell inside the cup, if it overflowed or not, The Diamond's tears remained.

Sometimes when The Diamond cried, alone in the rain, he saw her skin change from its golden amber to green, to blue to red and to white, weapons and lotuses dancing around her in circles, settling on a mace or a bow, and her tears would shine inside her eyes, and he knew she saw the universe then, only she did not know it.

What had he done to deserve her? Likely nothing, but perhaps the shame of his existence was finally getting paid in full. It was magpie's pay, but then it had been, by most standards, a magpie's life, one who's intimate details he couldn't share, any more than he could divulge The Diamond's secret even and especially to herself. More. He needed more. She was a lonesome, fragile thing, but if she knew she would leave and why wouldn't she? And what would be left of him then? Sores and lesions, and a trail of rotten fiend droppings leading back to a baby boy who might have known better.

A scream pierced the rainy night, instantly shattering his world and pain painted daydreams, and inside the cup, the silverfish tears lined up like a compass and pointed towards the direction he had come from.

He rose in a panic and slammed his head against the roof of the hole, knocking the cup over. The tiny needle of tears landed in a puddle and darted upstream, leading him towards the screams.

THE DIAMOND

Her sandaled feet glided over the puddles, and the wind kept the rain away from her in a halo. She was happy. Her mother had ruffled her hair and her sister, her usually grumpy sister had let her hug her. She had seen other parents doing that to their children, and had wondered if it was chide or love. Now she knew it was love, but little did she know...

The dokans around the hole were closed, the grey sheet metal curtains pulled down, covered with slogans towards the next election that some mastan or another would rob for his party. There were candles dancing in the window of the small masjid. So many eyes like the ten heads of Ravana, a whisper of the desert sands that had blown over the world with Allah's winds of monsoon.

She knew pain and sadness, the bundled emotions slowly dissolving in her race to help her mother, but fear is not the same. Apprehensive as she was at the unsavvy company of the hole, she did not truly know the forever-chilling kiss of fear. And as such she showed no caution. Such is the curse of love. It isn't blind but blinds, and worse for the willful, and oh did she want to love in that moment and never weep again.

She didn't hear the steps. She had an alertness others had shed, a feeling for energy that should have raised every hair on the back of her neck like a spider, but she was blind and only felt the bony fingers as they lewdly touched her spine. A touch that only lasted an eternity, less than an instant, and she screamed for the first time. A wail that sent the rain pouring upwards and swallowed the wind, blowing out the candles of the masjid, and plunged the world into darkness.

She screamed again, and over and again as strong hands clasped on her shoulders and spun her into the soundlessness of terror, the stench of rotting teeth, and the redolence of acrid sweat. Another hole, deeper and darker than her tiny den, drawing her in with the relentlessness of a recurrent nightmare, the hidden part of oneself that tugs when you're the weakest.

Trapped, she thought she would never cry or smile again, that there would never be another light, and in that instant, there was a flash of lightning, a roll of thunder, and the whisper of a hundred slithers converging on her. A scream rose from the reeking hole, and then another, and the firm clamp on her scrawny shoulders loosened, and began to shake.

THE WHORES

The older whore sat in the hole, letting its squalor embrace her like the mischief she had plotted.

There is no thing stronger than a mother's love in the world, and just as light struggles darkness in a veil of twilight so does her love struggle against her scorn.

She knew that her young daughter was a thing to be

worshipped. That the goddess, beaten and raped, that she kept trapped so deeply, was in The Diamond as well. Yet that was her fear as well, see? That she lacked the strength to embrace the jewel inside herself all along, and scorn won the struggle again, by comforting her fears.

She knew the weakness in men, most of the many, and had chosen this one carefully. Some men would do anything, their illusion of strength the greatest weakness of all, the perversion of their minds and the flaccidity of their wands.

He would be where she had told him, waiting for that little piece of her soul that glowed as strongly as she stunk.

She waited in the silence of raindrops for the sign that would come, somehow still believing that even then there would be absolution for her if only she uncovered the secret that bonded The Dealer so tightly to The Diamond.

Her legs began to beat nervously under her shari, sending a twinkle of anticipation up her thigh and into her crotch that felt like youth, and a shrill shriek drew her, ever so cautiously, with the slowness of a beast stalking prey, out of her lair and into the night.

She followed the screams to where she knew they would come from. Reveling in The Diamond's fear. She knew he wouldn't be able to perform just yet, he would need time, he would need pain. Pain was his weakness, she would get there before anything truly happened, but just enough to break The Diamond's spirit so she would never shine against her old eyes so strongly again.

She saw their shadows, drawn in charcoal behind the curtain of rain. Lightning flashed and thunder rolled, and she saw something else, and knew she couldn't take a step towards her daughter. She fell on her hands and knees, watching The Diamond's tears flowing blue and breathtaking onto the ground, an exquisite disorder of light, and into the gods' own work, protecting their own. And she too, just as her older daughter, knew The Dealer, and The Diamond's secret.

THE DEALER

He followed the arrow of tears glowing more strongly than they ever had before. The screams, echoing through the night should have been enough to wake the world, but he knew better, and had known forever, for he had screamed as a child, and no one had heard.

There was a time when he had believed in the stories of the characters with hero figures. Tall, broad shoulder, fearless of heart, and ever alert to the misery of the innocent. But no hero had ever come for him. He had no figure, his lungs barely kept pace with his legs, but he would have to be that savior, if only he could be fast enough.

Now, understand that what we have here is no Hero. What we have is a Heroin addict, amongst other things. but in the eyes of the gods did it truly make a difference? He knew the gods to be selfish too, their endless battles, molding the world for thousands of years, were often petty, and sometimes wrong. It is a fine line between a god and a demon, and often a revolving door. He found an extra breath in that duality, a strength that toughened his resolve and balled his skinny hands into fists, and his teeth into the grin of a confidence long lost.

He ran past his hole with barely a glance, the bluish arrow of tears urging him forward. Another step, old lecher, they whispered at him. Another step, if it is your last.

A flash of lightning preceded a roll of thunder by just an instant, where two figures appeared lined in the purple afterglow of Indra's bolt. A tall, gaunt one, and his mind almost melted, it was so close to the old man who had made him do things as a boy, horrible things, things he had later done himself, hoping that from victim he would turn victor but had only made him more miserable, more empty inside.

His wife was there, but she wasn't helping. He knew her hatred of The Diamond, yet couldn't imagine she would stay there motionless, but in the wet darkness he couldn't see her fear, he didn't know that she couldn't approach, for surely she was as cursed as the monster holding their daughter, and wouldn't take another step.

In the clutches of the demon he saw her. His precious Diamond, screaming to eclipse the thunder. But there was something else, in the rumble in the clouds the demon was also screaming, dark, angry bellows that held no strength, and another flash of lightning burned.

The arrow of tears had stopped, and in its place hundreds of snakes converged upon the monster, covering him from head to toe, but leaving The Diamond unharmed. He dropped to his knees.

"Vishahara," he whispered, recognizing Manasa's work in protecting his daughter, launching her army of snakes at her attacker.

They writhed through his hair, and over and under his clothes, running up and down his legs under his lungi, finding their way into his nose, his ears, his throat, and into and around the dark sweaty places he had intended to torment The Diamond with. He clawed at his eyes as The Diamond fell back, crying, her face a shining blue curtain, and every tear that hit the ground attached itself to a snake, glowing with the same vibrancy as herself, as they filled the monster's stomach, tripped his feet from under him, and sent him to the ground a broken shivering mass.

"Om Hreem Shreem Kleem Aim, Mansa Divyai Namah! Om Hreem Shreem Kleem Aim, Mansa Divyai Namah! Om Hreem…"

The Dealer picked up a heavy stone and walked up to the writhing monster, and brought the stone down on the man's face, over and again, no longer seeing him, no longer hearing the sobbing of his daughter that had subsided at his sight, but seeing only the toothless old man in the forest so long ago. His perverted eyes and beak of a nose. His rotting teeth and wrinkled face, and the stone smashing away into it. Crushing his skull into a pulp as he had wished so many times before. Dreamed even in his nightmares that he had had the strength to do it then. Praising Mansa Devi for allowing him his revenge now, even after all the years, and saving his daughter.

THE DIAMOND

"Abba! Abba!" She whispered gently, crawling away from the blood turning the rainwater red, her father's face smeared in it, his eyes alight, more alert than she had ever seen them before. There were demons that received a boon whenever a drop of blood hit the ground, but this monster was no demon. She knew this now, and some of the terror in her spine faded, seeing him bleed, covered in snakes that glowed with her tears.

Her mother was there too, kneeling, her eyes averted from the carnage, but even then she couldn't let herself imagine the worse and mistook her fear for reverence. Her father who loved her. Her father the hero she had believed him to be when, too young to tell the difference he still held the appearance of a giant, strong and caring for her like he cared for nothing else. Her mother who had come, and seen the miracle and worshipped.

Only her sister was absent, but she didn't worry about that yet, or at all as we'll find out, relieved as she was at her short lived fright.

Again, it was love, it's ugly joyful head rearing with the face and temper of Kumbhakarna. The caress of her mother's hand in her hair, her sister's impatient tolerance of her needful hug. Blinded she had been and blinded she remained. The Diamond was all the goddesses in one, but now Parvati shone strongest, and just as Mirza and Sahiba had believed they could love each other forever, she stared at her relatives oblivious to their selfish manipulations, seeing only what wasn't there.

Her father picked her up and hugged her. Blood staining her face and dress, kissing her hands and feet, and weeping silently to himself. She felt his tears mixing with hers, but again failed to see that when this happened they lost their glow.

Her heart stomped; somewhere deep beneath the city it activated small cracks in the ancient fault line. Immortality is ever only one heartbeat away, an echo of the life one lived that lingers on. Her heart connected everything and everyone. Sometimes when she caught her breath, there was a short lapse in time, and somewhere, someone dying had a brief instant of relapse, a second more to hold a love one as they passed. An instant to say: I...and never finish their sentence, because she wouldn't need to.

The Diamond held a love that knew no words and no shape. She just was, and in that moment, as the snakes slithered away, their work done, she was the wind and the rain, the earthquake and the thunder, the rumble of an empty stomach, the crystalline of an infinite note on the vibrato of a heart that knew too little to be wounded.

The Dealer's skeletal arms lifted her off the blood soaked ground, tenderly and carried her over to her mother.

"Bring her home." She heard him say, as her mother's feet shuffled from under her shawar kamiz, and grabbed her hand, turning her back on the carnage, and into the night.

THE WHORES

It's truly an amazing thing, how the motions of the universe can hold different meanings. Evil, greedy meanings, but amazing nonetheless.

There was something awed in the way her mother looked down on The Diamond. Something awed and hungry. If you've known true hunger you know that it consumes entirely, it burns through reason and soul to find its way into unfathomable pits, pits where one dare not look for fear of who they'd find there. Their true self, barren and naked and yearning and merciless. She had been hungry all her life. Truly through no fault of her own, life had just never fed her what she had needed, and she had faced the abyss so many times she held no fear of it anymore. She had let that darkness in, and let it mold her shriveled soul as the hole had shaped her spine.

The tears. She had seen The Diamond's tears and that glow illuminated the pit, but never to its depths, only enough for her to want more, to want to bask in the light, to feed her until the pit was a rainbow and it burst through her eyes. The Dealer and The Diamond's little secret was a secret no longer, but she needed more. Perhaps she was more like her husband than she admitted to herself. Perhaps that was why in spite of all the sorrow she had stayed in the hole, because she had there a kindred soul. The Diamond's tears had awakened the fiend hiding in all of us, the fiend that was the darkness, the fiend that was the pit, the fiend that she had drank and fucked away hoping it stayed buried.

"Asho," she whispered at her daughter, leading the little girl away. "Come."

They reached the hole, and found her older daughter waiting, her eyes as ravenous as her own, staring at the little jewel with the glow of the tiger's on a hunt. The eyes of a predator, but who in their monstrosity had ever felt themselves to be a monster?

They turned to walk away from their den, followed by the exhausted Diamond, her hand firmly caught in her mother's.

"Amu," The Diamond asked her usually bright voice a weary squeak, "kothay jacho?"

Her mother didn't look at her. "We're going somewhere near. Somewhere you can rest better than this old hole…"

"But Amu, my bed is here," The Diamond pleaded wearily. "Are we going to where you and appa spend your nights?"

Her mother laughed, and her sister turned, answering her with a smirk. "No little Diamond. Somewhere far better."

THE DEALER

He hadn't buried anyone in a long while, but then neither had he murdered, and had taken to it with youthful glee.

There was something exhilarating about it, the blood rushing to his temples, the tendrils of electricity coursing through his limbs, the metallic stench of the monster's blood filling his nostrils until it was his whole world.

The kill was as good as any high he had ever felt. Better, much much better. Death filled him with life, and his weak heart felt light, his shoulders relieved of the pain he had carried. When he thought back to the tragedy of his younger years, he could no longer remember it, only the trees and the stench of jackfruit, and the rising breeze that sang of rain. If only it were true and we'd have a very different man standing before us. Or no man at all, who knew what life had been robbed from him, and where his own would have taken him?

He threw the last shovelful of dirt with his hands over the body laying facedown in a ditch behind the mosque.

Someone would find it, but who would claim it? Certainly no one, and the police wouldn't bother to write a report. They would probably cheer that their daily burden had been lightened by one.

The rain had stopped, and the skies had cleared lighting his cadaverous face. The Diamond's tears had dissolved in the puddle of blood. He picked up the blood-soaked rock and carried it away, making his way back to the hole.

When he heard no voices and smelled no cooking as he approached, the first alarm bell rang and he ran towards his home, shaking.

The hole was empty, as any hole should be, save for this one, but neither his wife nor daughters were anywhere to be found.

Had his wife seen the tears? Where had his older daughter been? He had been about to enter his secret lair the moment he heard the scream, and his wife had already been there, too scared to intervene. How would she have known where to go? Had she feared the snakes would turn on her? Why would they? Unless...

Realization dawned on him when he bashed the monster's face. He had underestimated his wife and daughter one time too many, and now they had The Diamond.

He gathered the last of his murderous energy and dashed towards his lair behind the temple.

THE DIAMOND

Pain, her whole world had become pain. There are few things worse than the epiphany of love denied, then embraced and crushed by betrayal.

Tied inside the hole she couldn't understand what had happened and what she had seen, what she had felt. So real and everlasting, ending in a litany of lashes from those she had unwittingly believed in, beating her for what poured out of her body so freely from the heavens. The blessing that she was, manipulated for gain.

She looked at her tears turned diamonds, resting on the ridges lining the wall, the beauty of them, incandescent and true, all she had ever wanted them to be, turned into the opposite of her dreams. Objects of more want, of more misery, of more pain.

But worse was the anger and ecstasy of her mother and sister, their futile attempts to alleviate their pain with her tears, and the guilt she felt for causing it all.

They couldn't collect them all, they waded in them, tears the crystal blue of The Diamond's beauty of The Diamond's love for a world she could never know, flowing passed them in a river down the endless other pit where fault lines met and angels sung. Her tears slipped into the rift, slowly parting the old plates, eroding them, reviving the rivalry they had left behind.

She prayed even in her pain. Om. Om Nama. Om. For her fatherFor the Peace Corps teacher. For everyone and anyone. But the hole was deeper than her home, deeper than anything in the world. The depth of her crying soul.

How much have you cried, reader? Ask yourself, how much have you lost? How much have you bled and maybe you will know, the pain of that little girl.

It was then that her father crawled in, but his eyes weren't for her and she truly stopped believing then. But could never stop crying.

They hung at each others' throats, The Whores and The Dealer, not caring which was which. Only the tears mattered, only the diamonds, drowning in a flood that was never theirs to begin with.

Her tears hardened against her infant immortality, they flowed from one cave to another, crystalizing her toes first, and then her ankles, and then her knees till her fingertips became a reflection of pure passion, and finally sealing her throat until she couldn't breathe. The Diamond who could have been so much, filling the fault line a drop at a time. Glowing blue and frozen as a statue, her fingertips forming tara mudra, thumb and ring finger connecting in the absolute balance of meditation.

She wanted to yell at them. To yell at herself. But couldn't any longer, and never would, her eyes sealed forever, under a sheen of heavenly blue.

There was a rumble from down under, the earth answering her loss from eons of collisions that had berthed the mountains she so loved, yearning to be one with her.

The fault line broke. Unable to contain itself.

The temple collapsed on them all, reclaiming the love that was never meant to be.

EPILOGUE

There is a place in Dinajpur, where there used to be a temple. If you dig beneath it, if you have the guts to, you will find something else, a statue with the look of the ancients, and spread around it, old bones, and maybe a skull or two. Either one would make your fortune, but either one might also curse you...

If you dig and find them, be you blessed enough to do so, don't sell one and leave the other. Take them all as one, and bury them together, because they belong together, the bones and the statue, because like all of us they share a story, they share an understanding, a love and a pain, and like all of us, they are beautiful.

POPOBAWA

INTRODUCTION

Ahmad Tandika @ahmad_tandi.... 19h ago
  Dey r coming 2 get me. Dey r armed. I have no where 2 go.
  ...

Ahmad Tandika @ahmad_tandi.... 19h ago
  Help me. Please. Call da police. I am in Stone Town, by
Mercury house. Please. Help.
  ...

Ahmad Tandika @ahmad_tandi... 18h ago
  Da police is with dem. Dey outside. Dey have machetes and
axes. Dey chanting: popobawa! Popobawa!
  ...

Ahmad Tandika @ahmad_tandi... 18h ago
  Help. Help. Help.
  ...

Ahmad Tandika @ahmad_tandi... 17h ago

Dey have broken in. Dey coming up. No help is coming. Dey r hacking the door. Y? I have done nothing. Nothing at all.

CHAPTER 1

The onlookers stepped onto the balcony from their apartment, adding to the buzz coming from candlelit windows where shadows betrayed more nosey neighbors. Inspector Gurnah looked down, there was nothing he could do about them, and, as he had been reminded recently, he wasn't paid to check out the living.

"Go back inside! The police is working here! Sorry Inspector Gurnah, they're the neighbors who reported the crime, sir."

"Have you thanked them for their cooperation Benjamin?"

"Yes, sir."

Gurnah's stomach lurched in his throat. "These people will stop at nothing," he said, stepping out of the blood leaking from the two bodies lying discarded on the ground by one of Stone Town's oldest buildings. Life had been so quiet up to now, so, so quiet...

"Kuchu are not people sir," his adjunct, Benjamin, responded. "No normal person would do this, we should arrest them all, deport the Ugandans back to where they belong, and kill the local kuchu ourselves."

Inspector Gurnah nodded silently. It was one thing for the gay community to find refuge on the island, another to let them commit atrocities. And they had been warned. Multiple times. What was it the American pastor had said? Worse than Nazis?

Perhaps he had been right, and they should treat them the way the Nazis would have.

He still had a tight rein on things. The press was slow in these parts, it was so dark at night that even a thrill-seeking teen on a smart phone hadn't managed to snatch a shot, but word would start spreading eventually, and that would mean less tourists, less money to the island, and when that started happening there would be trouble. Perhaps he should all let it go to shit anyway.

"Make sure you don't say that whenever we start getting media attention. It's hard enough to keep things quiet as it is, don't wanna look like we're bending the law any more than we're already blamed for."

It's easy for people to use the word corruption when they're not underpaid. When they don't have to wake up to check out corpses, and deal with South African junkies and their nasty habits.

His adjunct's elbow hit him in the ribs. "Sir. Those damned nuns again."

Inspector Gurnah sighed and turned. Street lights barely made it all the way down to the corners, but he knew what he was looking for, a chubby short shape walking next to a tall thin one, heads wrapped and bodies covered in blue and white dresses. Walking with a self-righteous step and looking down their noses at him any chance they could. He hated Catholics with a passion, except Jesus. Because Jesus was dead.

These two nuns were nice enough, snootiness aside, but this was also complicated enough. No point dragging the occult into this, but his orders had been clear: be courteous and let them check out the scene. They are influential among the HIV positive community, if you show cooperation they will help avoid riots.

"Sister Okala! Sister Lukyamuzi! "How good to see you!" Inspector Gurnah said sarcastically as they approached.

Sister Okala snorted and sister Lukyamuzi smiled, pushing her glasses up on her nose and said,, "thank you Inspector. Maybe one day we'll meet in happier circumstances."

"I can't imagine a happy circumstance I would ever meet a sister in; Sister Lukyamuzi, in my experience they're either there to chastise you, or bury you." Inspector Gurnah said.

"Sorry for your shoe." Sister Okala added, pointing at the bloody footprints on the ground. "It's unwise to wear leather to a crime scene."

Sister Josephine Lukyamuzi held back a sigh and a smirk. Sister Innocent Okala lacked proper filters. You'd think that after thirty odd years serving the Lord Christ she would know better, but age had only made her fatter and bolder.

Inspector Gurnah either ignored her snide, missed it entirely, or didn't care at all. "The job doesn't wait, sister, and it's a messy job. But please don't let me get in the way of you doing yours."

Innocent nodded at him and they both stepped up to the bodies.

A young man and a young woman lay face down on the floor in a puddle of their own blood, their anuses torn open through their pants and skirt, intestines leaking through a hole in their abdomens, filling the air with the smell of liquid shit, blood, and something that you only find at crime scenes and need a keen nose to detect; the acrid sweat of terrified surprise, seeping out of their pores.

"That's a couple," Josephine said, "married too. They're wearing matching rings."

He shrugged. "And?"

Innocent pinched her nose bone, "Don't you find it strange that a gay serial killer would anally rape both a man and a woman?"

He shrugged again. "Who knows what kind of unnatural urges those people act upon. The first two victims were both men, plus he didn't fuck her in her pussy did he?"

Abdulkader Gurnah wasn't the most sophisticated officer they had met. But arguing his point was pointless. "True," Innocent said. "But what if the next victim is a woman? Why do this to a couple when he, if it is a he, could have gone to a club to find a victim? What did the neighbors say?"

"Same thing they did last time. They heard wings beating, then they heard screams, and by the time they came out, the bodies were on the floor stinking up the street."

"Your suspect is a fast one isn't he?" Nun Josephine said. "A quick roll in the hay, do you think you could be that fast?"

Both officers shot her a dark glance.

"You insinuating something, sister?" Gurnah asked.

"Not at all officer, not at all," Josephine said, "Only that your suspect didn't seem to take the time to enjoy his victims very much. Odd, don't you think? And for the third time, your guy would be one hell of a stallion. He literally drilled them through to the other side of their bodies. Again. I can't speak from experience..."

"I can," Innocent said. "But I was another person back then."

"I can't speak from experience," Josephine continued, "But I doubt most men could do this."

Another shrug. "Again, who knows what motivates these perverts. And...And this is a technical point, sisters, police jargon so to speak, but we don't have a suspect at this point, only very dead bodies."

Innocent took Josephine by the arm, leading her away from the crime scene. "You don't have a suspect inspector... but we do."

CHAPTER 2

Standing on a rooftop nearby, James Matonge looked down at the two nuns walking away. The night was moonless but it made no difference to him. He could see as if it was broad daylight although he couldn't remember daylight. He couldn't remember that he was James. Which at the present moment was a good thing. All he knew was that his dick was covered in blood and still throbbing, all he could remember were the two dead bodies' thoughts.

He was an engineer, she was a school teacher. They had met in high school and had loved each other since, although she had hated him at first. He had thought he would become a soccer player, she had thought she would be a singer. He had grown up with six brothers and sisters and had a scar on his left shoulder from playing soccer with his older brother when he was eight. She was an only child when she had hurt herself for the first time. She had never gotten over losing her mother to a car accident when she was six. Both were scarred in different ways, both had been madly in love.

The memories pained him. He felt them as if they were his own, and in many ways they were. For the time being they were the only memories he had left, and he wept silently, wept at the loss of his loved one, wept at his childhood memories blurring into each other, mingling into one single throbbing pulse of pain, and took off from the roof into the night.

"Hello sisters." Kona Shio said, his voice shaking, his eyes heavy with tears, his hair unkempt, and his cheeks marked with scratches from his own nails still covered in dry blood. "Thank you for coming."

The parade was muted and somber. Only four people were carrying the coffin, and a few of his close friends quiet under the streetlights, to avoid drawing any attention. Innocent couldn't imagine how that must feel, she had tried many times but never could. A flawed individual for sure, but a beating heart just the same as hers, as everybody's, and she was not perfect either. No one was.

She put a comforting hand on his shoulder and he trembled. "Of course we came, Kona," Innocent Said, "of course we did."

He rested his head on her hand, weeping. "I loved him so much," he said softly. "So, so much."

"We know," Josephine said. "Ahmad was a great guy."

"No one came to help him. No one," he whispered, following the coffin. "It's my fault. My phone was off. I was out drinking. We'd just had a fight. I was never going to leave him, but I had to step out, to breathe, to take my mind off things. Why, sisters? What had he done? I could have come. I could've helped."

"There was nothing you could have done," Innocent said. "There was nothing he could do. Neither of you. If you had come you would be dead too."

"At least we'd be dead together," he said. "They hacked him to pieces sisters. And then hacked the pieces to pieces, they stuck his cock into his own ass and left him there, blood, everywhere, blood, so much of it..."

Sisters Josephine and Innocent looked at each other. They had seen and heard worse before leaving Kampala for Zanzibar, but it was horrible each time. Worse each time, and it never seemed to end.

The procession broke through the buildings and onto a thin strip of sand lit with candles leading to the waters and a small fishing boat, a little ways away from the busy harbor and the tourists' yachts reminding them of how insignificant they were.

They approached the small boat and lowered the coffin, tied off the knot, pushed it into the water and set it on fire.

No cemetery would have Ahmad's body but they would return him to nature in one form or another.

———

"So, what do we have?" Innocent asked, as they swept the floor of Christ Church cathedral in Stone Town. The multicolored lights illuminating the statues of the saints in the alcove.

"What do you mean, what do we have?" Josephine asked back. "Just because we know what it is, doesn't mean we know who it is, and that's the problem."

"Solving this was never why we came Josephine. It's a boon if we can, but we still have the clinic to run and the outreach. We're getting old, we can't keep running around all night and working all day."

"If we don't solve this there won't be a clinic left to run. The mobs will get worse. They'll kill off the whole community or they will flee again, and we're too old to keep following. And what for? The creature will follow them too. It's smart, it knows exactly how to disguise its crimes."

"It is getting sloppy though," Innocent pointed out. "Until now it only attacked men, that changed yesterday. Even in Kampala, the victims were men, easy pickings for the mob."

"Wouldn't have happened if it weren't for the witch hunt. You know that."

"I don't know that. All I know is we're running out of options, and health."

"Alright then. Let's think this through. What do we know?"

They'd had this conversation before, once in Kampala after David Kato had been murdered with a hammer and the police had blamed it on a disgruntled lover, as if one man could swing six hammers at once. And again the same conversation in Dar es Salaam when they'd decided they'd come here, to Zanzibar, following the Ugandan gay community seeking refuge on the island where Freddie Mercury was born and raised.

They'd thought people here would be sympathetic to their cause. They'd been wrong.

Josephine could give Innocent as much crap as she wanted, perhaps if she ate more herself she wouldn't be so tired all of the time and her knees would be healthier. Or maybe not. Maybe they were just old. Two old nuns trying to do right by the Lord.

"We know this has nothing to do with lust," Josephine said. "We know what creature is responsible. We know that it operates at night. We know that it has wings. We know that it changes back into a human by day. We don't know who that human is. We don't know how to find him. The only thing certain is that it can't kill us because we believe in it. No one else on the island does. Anyone can be a victim. And the more attention it gets the more likely it will leave Stone Town."

"We only have one option left," Innocent said with tired eyes. "Patrolling the streets ourselves until something gives. I don't know if I can remain faithful if God doesn't allow us to slay this beast."

Josephine nodded. She felt the same way. Perhaps every person of faith did at some point or another. It wasn't something anybody wanted to discuss, not when you felt the ground turning to jelly beneath your feet, your already feeble knees buckling under the weight of your soul and a burden often too heavy to bear. She had seen it in even the most irreproachable in the church, a flicker in their eyes that revealed more than they thought. Perhaps this was their test. An odd an awful test, but maybe just a test as of yet.

"Agreed."

"Agreed."

The clinic was full. Every bench occupied, every wall lined with patients. They were doing God's work, but sometimes it felt like He was stingy with recruiting staff. Nonetheless, Josephine still loved the job.

Funny the things you're told about addicts until you meet one, and realize that they're no demons, they're much quieter, much more sober people, self-righteous and judgmental people could be much worse, so much worse.

The only problem was, in almost a week, they had made no progress, and there had been one more victim.

"How are you feeling today, Husna?" Josephine asked.

"I'm OK, Sister Lukyamuzi. Thank you. I stayed busy today, it helps keep the withdrawal away but I'm still struggling with the new hours you keep."

They had heard this for several days now. The HIV patients didn't complain too much, as long as they received their medication regularly, but the heroin addicts had a harder time. If they didn't get their methadone on time the local dealers were quick to fill in the gap with a discounted dose, knowing it would only take one to get them back on the train hurtling a thousand miles an hour back into addiction.

The nuns didn't have a choice. With their new schedule, neither Innocent nor Josephine could make it to work in the morning, and they needed to patrol together. It meant that there would be a line around the block where the clinic was located, and most of the patients would be upset, irritable and ready to snap at them. But they still came, that's what mattered, they still came and continued their treatment, changed their needles daily, took their opioid substitution seriously.

"I know, Husna," she said, handing her a dose of blue methadone in a white paper cup, watching her snatch it hungrily and gulp it down. "We're old ladies you know," she said, laughing heartily. "Soon we'll need you to give us pills." Husna laughed at that. "Are you staying for the group discussion?"

"Of course, Sister Lukyamuzi. Of course. Talking makes me feel better. Sister Okala also spoke of a center in town where they needed a cleaning lady. Do you think she can still help me?"

"Of course she can. I'm very proud of you, Husna. We both are. Grab a seat I'll call her for you."

"Sister!" Abdallah, another patient, called impatiently, lounging against the wall. He was always impatient and the user she worried most about, the most easily swayed by the dealers' swan song.

"One minute there, Abdallah, I'll be right back, and don't let me catch you trying to sneak behind the counter now, you hear?"

"Don't worry sister," Husna said. "I'll keep an eye on him for you."

Abdallah laughed as she walked away. "Ha! Husna, pretty lady. I have my eyes on you."

Josephine walked down the small hallway lined with posters on drug prevention and safe sex recommendations, passed the examination room where applicants for opioid substitution, HIV and Hepatitis C screenings lay on small white beds, and into the common room where Innocent was helping a young teenager work his way through windows 98, looking about to lift the screen off the table and bash his head in with it.

"Akeem, I swear to you. If you don't focus I will carve a target out of your face and use it for shooting practice…"

"Innocent!" Josephine snapped.

"What?! The kid is useless."

Akeem grinned and rubbed his head. Josephine shook her own.

"Never mind. Husna is here, she wants to know about the job you promised her."

"Ah! Finally someone showing progress," Innocent said, hugging Akeem. "You keep trying, kid. You'll get there."

Some days were good days.

CHAPTER 3

James turned and twisted in his sleep. He had tried everything but couldn't sleep until the early hours of the morning. Getting blind drunk was one of those things, but he had only managed to throw up. He had dosed himself with Xanax, sleeping pills and Oxycodone, to no effect, and when sleep finally came, the dreams started again.

Sometimes they were good. Most times they were abominable, distorted pictures of the reel of memories he had tried to bury and burn as a child, thirty years ago.

Today they were good, but too vivid and penetrating all the same. His little sister was holding his hand, and they were heading towards the market, barefoot on the dirt road leading away from their village, the grass on either side of them lush under the blackish-grey and cloudy skies of the rainy season. But it wouldn't rain until afternoon. Somewhere above them, the clouds were drinking their fill, drinking to burst, and if they weren't home by noon the curtain of rain would fall so thick it drowned the world.

Jendyose was skipping ahead now, laughing, strands of her unusually straight hair raising in a thin crown around her head with the static of the oncoming storm. She wasn't usually this lively, not anymore. Their father must have wandered in drunk last night and passed out.

"Not so fast!" he yelled after her, but she just pulled her tongue out at him and giggled, skipping away even further, her blue dress flapping in the gently rising wind, revealing her scrawny legs that somehow never seemed to tire, and she disappeared over the bend of the hill, running down its flank with utter abandon.

He ran up to catch her, ran down until he was inches away, picked her up, and rolled with her in the damp grass, the two of them laughing as they had when they were smaller, as they seldom did anymore.

Today was a good day, and it wouldn't rain until later.

He looked up from his sister's hair, a winged shadow making its way across the sky. It caught sight of them and plunged towards them, one dark, red eye open.

James woke up panting and sweating, the room around him thinning, and darkness closing in on him.

It was a small crowd, but it had all the foreboding of a snowflake turning into a snowball at the very top of a mountain. The avalanche would come.

"Give us the kuchu!" someone yelled.

"All of them!" a woman standing in front of the mob said. Her eyes shining with barely held rage.

"The others can go! But the kuchu stay with us!" a dark and chubby man yelled.

Sisters Okala and Lukyamuzi had expected them sooner. It had been three days since the last corpse was found, bleeding, reeking and raped The press was there too, standing aside, filming and taking shots of the half dozen angry would be mob, speaking with all the authority of halfwits with clubs, confident but not smart or prepared enough to know what they were doing.

Innocent stepped up to them, while Josephine turned the key to the lock, caught into the thick chain keeping the heavy, metal doors of the clinic shut. They knew what running a medical center like theirs meant. There were no windows giving out on the streets, only onto the central courtyard. The bathrooms were ventilated; the only access was through the door or a forty-foot drop from the roof.

"There is nobody here but us," Innocent started. "And by the looks of you I could take you all down myself."

The journos laughed at that, pens scratching her quote frantically on their note pads.

"You lucky you're women of God, otherwise…" one of the men started.

"…or you'd run to clean up your rooms like you did for your mothers?" Innocent finished.

The reporters laughed some more. The men and women in the crowd looking increasingly confused.

"Again. There is no one here," Josephine said walking up to the crowd. "Even if there were, we wouldn't let you have them."

While the last bit was true, the first was not. A dozen patients were hiding inside, with enough food and drinks to last the night. She had locked the opioid supplies, but in their frightened state she expected some of them to break into the storage room anyway. But better to deal with that, than with more innocent corpses.

It was almost nightfall. There was something more menacing about a crowd at night no matter how small, something about the anonymity of darkness that made them more daring, bolder, but now they looked subdued between the stoniness of the nuns and the smirking of the press.

"You can't protect them forever, sisters," a tall dark woman said pushing her way passed two men. "And you can't protect them everywhere," she said and walked away.

Josephine and Innocent looked at each other, not quite sighing in relief, not before the press, but the woman's words were all too true. They couldn't be everywhere, and certainly not forever. As one they turned towards the trailing journalists.

"And you! Don't you have some real news to report?!"

CHAPTER 4

Labyrinths are not mythical places, they are real places, built not to entrap, but born as a testimony to the chaos of life. There are no more straight paths through a forest than through a city. Every bump changing the outline into a map of what used to be.

Stone Town was one of those mazes. A mess of tiny streets lined with ancient buildings of coral stone, reddish grey walls laced with the marks of time and change. Old Arab and Indian carvings clashing against small stores where only bicycles could fit, intricately designed verandas and a mix of people tying three continents together, slaves, imams and subcontinental merchants creating a harmony that existed nowhere else.

Making their way through the moonless streets, Innocent and Josephine had no mind for the wonder around, only for the horror at bay, their footsteps slow and determined, their eyes and ears focused on the shadows, on the lookout for the beating of wings and screams.

"What time is it now?" Innocent asked.

"Almost three."

"We should make it back to the clinic. Just in case."

Josephine shook her head. "We've done all we can, they can't break through, and if anybody sees us go in they will rush their way in with us. We have to keep going. We just have to."

"I know but..."

<<< >>>

Piercing dread tore him out of his sleep.

Please stop screaming. Please stop. He thought.

The room was dark and damp. He wanted to light the candle, step out into the hallway and do something, but he was scared to. He so wanted the screams to stop but knew that something worse came after the screams. He was too young to know what, but saw it in her eyes in the morning; the vacant stare, the cringing back the moment he reached out to take her hand and walk her to school.

She would hide and sob, and pummel his face with her tiny fists when he would find her. It was always the same thing. Every day or close enough. And he did nothing about it. The worst was that he would fall asleep again after the screams stopped, while it would be a sleepless night for her...

>>> <<<

"...what just happened?!" Innocent asked, scanning the empty street. "Did you feel that? Did you..."

<<< >>>

There was dried blood on her lip that morning, and a bruise on her cheek, and so many more he couldn't see hidden under her dress.

He looked up at his mother imploringly, but she didn't look back, her eyes darting over them laden with shame.

Why didn't she do anything? How could she let this happen?

Jendyose sat at the table, her bowl of millet untouched, swaying with fatigue and pain. He reached a hand out to her but she pulled back with a yelp, looked at him, and started crying...

>>> <<<

Josephine had stopped walking, her eyes darting around as well. But the street was empty. "I did," she said. "I was in a small bedroom, alone, and there were screams. Innocent did you hear the screams?"

"I wanted the screams to stop." Innocent answered. "I was so ashamed but I needed them to stop. I wanted to go back to sleep and needed them to stop, maybe if I slept…"

Josephine's mind was coming back but the look in her mother's eyes…

Not my mother, she thought, that was not my mother, that wasn't me at all. I never had a sister, I have never seen these people…

She reached over and hugged Innocent who wept uncontrollably. Her usually boisterous companion reduced to a shuddering mass of tears and snot.

"What was that, I…"

<<< >>

"Hey, Jen, hey, look at me plea…"

>>> <<<

The walls and street started merging into a dirt road and green hills. Josephine pushed them away, feeling her heart burst as if she were running a marathon, blood rushing to her temples, her eyes bulging in their sockets. But it worked, the dirt around her feet turning back to solid stone pavement.

Innocent stared blindly ahead.

Josephine caught her by the shoulders shaking her violently. "You can control it!" she yelled, still shaking her friend.

Innocent's eyes regained focus, looking at her desperately.

Then there was a scream.

They chased the echoing scream down dark alleys.

"It can't be far!" Josephine yelled at Innocent, trailing a few yards behind her.

It wasn't just their age, with every step the waking dream tried to push through their consciousness, walls changed to trees, puddles and mud appeared ahead of them obscuring the road. But the screams made it through, piercing through reality and dream alike, shattering both.

"Focus Innocent! Focus!" she kept encouraging her friend,

unsure of whether she wouldn't trip and fall over an uneven pavement herself. They ran past a small mosque that for a moment was a muddy hill, and rounded the corner.

The dreams stopped, and for a moment she wished they hadn't, that she could hide in the velvety green canopy of the forest forever.

On the street running parallel to the mosque, the body of a young woman lay flat on her face, blood maculating her blond hair, leaking out of her ass and turning her blue jeans brown, guts squeezing their way under her armpits, seeping into the pavements and trickling to the stone walls of the mosque and the houses around it.

Not a local.

A white woman.

A tourist.

There would be no keeping the press out of this. This would go viral and there would be no stopping the mob.

Innocent caught up with her, panting, and gasped.

A sound caught their ear, the displacement of air from above their head pulled their eyes upward, and a pair of black wings disappeared behind the mosque.

CHAPTER 5

Strange events in Stone Town tonight.

The body of Heather Tandeski from Ottawa, in Ontario, Canada, was found by two local nuns, lying by the side of a mosque, in a pool of her own blood, brutally and viciously raped and murdered.

Heather had only been in Zanzibar for a few weeks, volunteering at a local high school as a volleyball teacher, and according to her friends had stayed late after meeting a local boy for a few drinks. The bartender reported having seen her leaving the bar alone, the young man still ordering drinks at the time of her murder.

While the two nuns declined any comment. Police Inspector Abdulkader Gurnah said the following: "This is not an isolated event. Heather is unfortunately the fifth victim in a series of similar occurrences. We do not have a suspect as of yet, but believe that the murders are somehow linked to the presence of hundreds of homosexuals who have moved to our beautiful island mainly from Uganda and mainland Tanzania.

We are investigating, but I urge people to avoid the streets of Stone Town late at night, or anytime passed sunset if possible. We also request members of the gay community to report to the precinct to be registered for their own protection."

"But Inspector Gurnah if you think so, why would two of the victims have been women?"

"Ha! Misdirection! But we will not be fooled Ms. Rahman. You can be sure."

"...yes. I'm sure Inspector Gurnah, very sure..."

Well, however the Inspector feels, it appears that word had already made it to the street. Only a week ago young Ahmad Tandika of Dar es Salaam was savagely murdered in his home by a group of local residents. A crime reminiscent of the attacks on the gay community in Uganda not so long ago.

The situation is bad, but might get even worse if the killings go on. Groups of local residents patrol the streets and beaches hungry for blood.

We wish the police the best in their efforts and a swift return to peace to beautiful Zanzibar.

Reshma Mojibur Rahman, reporting live for the BBC.

———

"And you just happened to be there?"

"No Inspector Gurnah, we live there. In Stone Town? We didn't just happen to be there."

"Sister Lukyamuzi. Don't you find it strange that the murders began in Kampala when you lived there, and now they follow you here?"

"If we did why would we tell you?"

"Yes. If we did why would we tell you?" Innocent fired in. The quiet of the precinct and the eyes of all the officers focused on them were making her nervous. "And the murders didn't follow us, we followed them."

"You're actually accusing us, of raping and murdering these people?" Josephine asked.

Inspector Gurnah laughed. "No! But you are too close to the kuchu. You must know something."

"We know they have nothing to do with this. You should come by the clinic, meet your jurisdiction." Innocent said.

"My jurisdiction is why you are being questioned. You are free to cooperate or not, but know that you will no longer be given access to our crime scenes. Two officers will guard your clinic and inspect the premises regularly in case something untoward is happening there," he said, raising his index finger, looking at the two nuns, and decided they didn't look contrite enough. "And don't let my men catch you at a crime scene again, or the conversation will be a lot worse."

"I doubt that." Josephine snorted.

"Please leave, sister Okala." Gurnah exhaled, his face in his palm, "Along with your colleague."

———————

"Haraka Kuchu! Haraka!"

A short chubby man in a pink shirt ran passed Inspector Gurnah and his adjunct on their way to lunch from the precinct.

Close behind were a group of children, no older than twelve, hurtling small rocks at him, one of them armed with a sling, hitting him on the back of the head, sending him slamming into a wall, spraying it with a small splatter of blood.

He turned around his eyes in shock, raising his hand to his skull and looking at the blood and bits of hair sticking to his fingers, and back at the children, who threw another volley of stones at him.

"What are they doing inspector?"

"Playing this new game Benjamin. It's called Run homo! Run! If they don't run fast enough they get stoned."

"Do we have enough rocks?"

"I hope so."

"What should we do about the nuns?"

"Nothing for now, just keep an eye on them…"

CHAPTER 6

James kept the darkness away. Never more than an inch from overwhelming the little sanity he had left, he had read about this, the guilt that never let you rest, how no matter how hard you tried, grief lingered in the little pockets of your soul and surged when you thought you'd forgotten, endlessly tying you back to the person you were on the chain gang of past and present.

It had been days now since he'd forgotten his nights. Days since the winged demon found its way into his reminiscences.

Alone in his windowless room, buckets on the floor filled with his urine and feces, too scared to take them out to find the creature waiting for him on his doorstep, the smells merged into the thick, warm haze of his decay. His fingernails torn and bloody from scratching his little sister's name into the walls.

He caught a glimpse of himself in the mirror.

He remembered another man looking back at him not so long ago, but it might have been years. Tall, handsome, strong. The image the mganga had shown him in the flames when he had begged for her help. That image had never materialized. Instead, the darkness had grown, enveloping all that he was, thin tentacles of vengeful malevolence that never found satisfaction, and kept drawing him in, one night at a time.

The man standing there held nothing of the child he once was, or the man he could have become. Dirty, sweating, hunched over, pants covered in stains of food, drink and vomit, eyes red with fatigue, emaciated ribs poking through his blackish-grey sickly skin, his heart visibly beating in his chest. He didn't know that man, but then he no longer truly knew himself.

There was a knock on the door.

"Who is it?!"

But no one answered, instead the door started rattling and shaking angrily. The darkness had returned.

"No! No please! Not again!" he implored crawling into a corner of his room between two buckets of his own waste. "Please, please not again."

The rattling stopped, and the slit between the door and the floor turned black, leaking the thick ooze of his curse into his room, like nails clawing the floor, inexorably, towards him.

———

Inspector Gurnah whistled as he walked down the street.

It was full moon, and the light found its way down to the pavements, bouncing along windows and reflecting on shiny stonework, until it hit the ground, casting lighter shadows into the dark corners of the scrawny pathways.

The streets had always helped clear his mind. Whether or not he reached the right conclusions was a matter of debate, but it gave him clarity of purpose. And this time was no different.

The ploy to have the local homosexuals register with the police was working. Too many were here illegally, and his team had turned over almost a hundred of them to immigration authorities and shipped them back to where they belonged. Others rotted in his cells. For their own protection, of course. It meant he couldn't detain regular street criminals anymore, but they were a common nuisance, not a threat to society.

He turned a blind eye to what happened in the interrogation rooms. He heard the screams sometimes. Policing couldn't always be pretty, and he needed results. Something had to give eventually, and he would be handed the killer on a platter. No one would complain about a few broken bones or rectums torn open with a baton after that. He would brush away the naysayers and point to the newly found calm in the streets, how tourists were returning to the island, how he had single handedly dealt a blow to an international conspiracy by western powers to turn local children gay.

If only he could do the same to the two nuns. They were meddlesome and useless, and they had to be in on this. They had to. Dammit they had to be. Who would spend so much time with such filth and not at least overhear something of value. They refused to cooperate, that alone should be enough, but go arrest a couple of nuns and he would never hear the end of it.

A large bird flew over him, casting its shadow on the sidewalk ahead of him.

Zanzibar was not a place where he had expected having to conduct such an intense investigation. Really, who in the world could...

<<< >>>

...The forest grew darker as he moved forward. The village elder had told him that he would find the mganga at the very heart of it. It was strange how it happened, one moment he was walking off the dusty road into the grove of trees, the moon still reflecting on his back and shining through the trunks and leaves ahead, fading slowly with each step. Then nothing.

He looked up through the branches and the moon was gone. Even the stars dotting the obscure canvas danced in patterns James had never seen before. He thought he knew all the stars and constellations, zuhura and the kilimia, twiga and ndoo kubwa, but he couldn't tell what he was looking at that night. As if he had taken one step too many through a forest on earth and stepped out on a distant world. He thought perhaps all the forests in the universe were connected and all the worlds through them, and shuddered at the immensity of it, at the possibilities.

Somewhere ahead a small flame broke the obscurity, a beacon in an otherwise alien world.

He approached cautiously, watching each step to avoid walking into a bush or a tree and found an old woman dressed in blue and green sitting behind a fire, before a mud hut with a thatched roof, rolling small shells into a hole dug in the ground in front of her, chanting quietly.

The heat from the fire drenched him in sweat almost at once, while the old woman seemed immune, not even a droplet showing on her smooth forehead, under a rich crown of white hair.

The door to the mud hut was open and the flames should have been enough to see inside, but the darkness in her small home seemed infinite, just as the forest around them. If he looked hard enough he could almost see another light dancing in the hut, as tiny as the fire ahead of him had seemed when he first noticed it.

The fire burned with a blue green flame. He expected to smell some kind of petrol, but instead the smoke smelled of nuts and fruit, of grass after the rain, of a woman's hair.

She waved him over, not bothering to look up, and with the same hand invited him to sit down before her.

He opened his mouth to speak, unsure of how to explain his coming, nervous about how to phrase his request.

"You are afraid," she said before he spoke. "But fear not for yourself."

"You are ashamed," she continued, "but not for what you have done but for what you have not."

James stared at her, fascinated. The shells' clicking growing faster as she rolled them over and again in front of her, glowing as they reflected the light from the fire, and with something of their own, as if an eye was open in each one of them, looking directly into him.

"I see the evil that she fears. I feel the pain you wish to stop. None so young should have to fear so much or carry such responsibility. Look into the fire I will show you something..."

>>> <<<

What the...Abdulkader thought, losing his footing, watching the fire disappear before his eyes to be replaced by a small merchant's cart. Where was I?

The beating of wings came again, and the sky above him darkened...

<<< >>>

"Are you sure?" she asked him as they sat, turning away from the fire.

"Yes!" he yelled, his voice carrying no further than the fire and the hut. "Yes! I am sure!"

She raised an eyebrow, looking up at him for the first time. "You are young, very young."

"I am the only one she has."

The mganga nodded. "Do you understand? Do you understand that if you fail to stop the evil, you will become the evil yourself? Cursed to perpetuate what you so loathe? Ruining everything that you have tried to do? The memory of she you want to save?"

James hesitated. He didn't dare intervene as it were. Would he have the determination to use the mganga's gift? He closed his eyes, thinking about the screams, about Jendyose's tiny hands rolled into fists, her nails cutting into her palms, her eyes squeezed shut, trying desperately to forget, to find the strength to take another breath.

"Yes," he said. "Yes. I understand."

"Very well," she said, handing him a small bowl, smelling of fermented fruit. "Drink it. Drink it to the last drop. Then enter the hut and follow the flame, it will take you back to the dirt road...."

The hut disappeared before him, the wings stopped beating, a large shadow landing behind him, the strength of a thousand men trapped in two powerful hands shoved him to the ground before he could scream, his teeth shattering against the pavement, two of them cutting deeply into his gums and pallet.

A burning pain ran through him as he felt his anus tearing open, his pelvis shattering and his abdomen exploding beneath him.

Innocent and Josephine rounded the corner onto the street, their minds still partially inside the mganga's hut walking towards what was not a flame but a door, miles away in the distance, and found Inspector Gurnah's corpse lying flat down, perforated from ass to stomach, pearly white teeth spread around his head like a crown.

They stared at each other. Averting their eyes from the corpse, a guilty sense of satisfaction spreading between them, that they tried to push down but as hard as they tried, they just couldn't.

"What should we do?" Josephine asked.

Innocent hesitated and gave the corpse a long, sad look. "This is sad, even if it's him. But he was clear wasn't he? Don't let me catch you near a crime scene."

Josephine nodded.. "Yes, he did say that, didn't he?

And they walked away.

He looked down at the young boy crying in the bathroom in front of him. Tears of pain and tears of shame flowing down his cheeks while Abdulkader pulled up his pants and tied his belt.

Euphrese wasn't the first younger teenager he had cajoled into the bathroom and forced to let him use sexually. No one knew about him so far, or at least no one spoke of it. Arusha was a place of veiled looks and quiet glances behind powerful laughter and luminescent smiles. None of the boys would talk, but someone would find out eventually, and he would have to leave, and then his family would carry the blame, so he decided Euphrese would be his last.

"It's ok," he said patting the sobbing teen on the shoulder. "It will be over soon."

He finished, pulling his pants down again.

It wasn't easy being married. Most days were fine. His wife had gotten used to his weird kinks during sex, or didn't voice her discomfort at any rate. And sometimes he would feel an urge, a longing, and would take it out on her emotionally, and sometimes, not often, but sometimes, physically. He hated himself when the urges came. That was the old him. The new him knew better, recognized his juvenile mistakes for what they had been, juvenile. And sometimes, when he couldn't contain them, he patrolled the neighborhoods of Dar es Salaam where the gays resided, and beat some of them up.

She was a good wife, she kept the house clean and food on the table, and although it wasn't fully love he felt for her, there was a love there of sorts, and that was all that he asked for. She let him be the man that he was, and he kept a roof over her head and living well. It was all she wanted. It was all he could ever give her.

James crawled back into his stinking den, the last of those

foreign memories fading with the disgust he felt while experiencing them, only to be replaced by even more sordid thoughts of his own.

He couldn't go on like this. Not much longer.

CHAPTER 7

"What is going on here?!"

"Let us through!"

Sister Okala and Sister Lukyamuzi pushed against the tide of people crowding the entrance to the clinic, some streaming in, others wading out, dragging their patients by their arms, legs and hair into the afternoon sunlight.

The patients made no sound, knocked unconscious or too terrified to yell, their eyes wide and vacant, as if they'd given up all hope and relinquished themselves to the whims of the crowd.

Dear Jesus. We should have seen it coming. Innocent thought. We should have known.

They made their way to the door, where the police officer on duty stood, his back against the wall, one leg folded up, a cigarette in hand and a grin on his face.

Josephine slapped the cigarette out of his hand. "What is going on? You were supposed to secure the location!"

His smile never faded and he picked up the cigarette. "Haven't you heard?" he said, blowing smoke slowly towards the sky, "Inspector Gurnah is dead. I have no one to take orders from anymore, and I am not paid to get quartered. Not for a bunch of kuchu and junkies."

Innocent punched him in the gut, he backhand slapped her across the jaw to the ground.

"I stayed here waiting for you," he said spitting next to her head, "But you don't need my protection do you? Handle this yourselves."

He stormed away, shoving the people and melting into the crowd.

Josephine helped Innocent up, almost buckling under her weight. "We have to go inside."

"I'm not sure I want to."

The crowd was dispersing, chanting: "Popobawa! Popobawa! Popobawa!" streaming like sewage into the tiny streets, dragging their unconscious victims behind them.

The clinic was ransacked, needles and glass littering the floor, tainted with trails of blood where the patients had been dragged out. The light bulbs were shattered too, graffiti covered the walls saying: death to the kuchu, and a string of profanity directed at the nuns, at god, at the world.

The medicine cabinet had been turned over and emptied of all its contents, methadone, anti-retroviral drugs, the safe was gone, and the address book with the names and address of all the patients who weren't at the clinic at the time. The slaughter had just begun, and there was no one to turn to. Not with the inspector dead, not with the whole city against them.

A muttered sound came from the examination room. Innocent and Josephine made their way there quietly.

Husna hung from the ceiling, her stomach pierced and bleeding thick droplets to the floor, building up in a small puddle beneath her. Next to her, Akeem, the teenager Innocent had worked so patiently with, hung there too, still alive, struggling against the rope crushing is neck.

"Quick!" Innocent yelled, "Help me take him down!"

Innocent grabbed Akeem by the legs, pushing his body up to relieve the pressure on his neck, while Josephine ran out to grab a chair and a piece of glass. "Hurry Jo! Hurry!"

Josephine rushed back in. Akeem weakly fighting death as she stood next to him, sawing against the rope, his breath slowing with each slice through the threads.

The rope gave away, Akeem's body sliding to the floor, exhaling one last relieved breath before he died.

The two nuns walked the night streets in a daze of crippling pain.

It enveloped them like a fever, warm, sweaty and pulsating with the steadiness of a heartbeat. The air itself felt thick with it, every breath hurt, every step. Even as they walked away from their life's work, the open door and unconscious bodies dragged through it seemed to pop out of every wall, every window was broken and every gust of wind sounded like two hanging corpses swaying in the wind.

The smell of smoke and melting glass drifted through the streets, it didn't smell like charred flesh, and they both took comfort in that, in anything they could, in the presence of each other, the only other person whom they could rely on for support, for understanding, for love.

"We have to leave Josephine," Innocent said, her voice distant, "we did what we could. It would be suicidal to stay."

Josephine nodded focusing ahead.

"We've done the best we could. You know that right? You have to know that."

"Maybe not," Josephine said and pointed ahead.

Across the street from them a young boy was stepping out of a moonlit forest, his hands glowing with a pink and blue light crackling along his fingers like lightning bursts, the glow growing more intense as he balled those hands into fists. His eyes glazed over with the steeliness of determination.

He walked through them, the boy who had felt so much pain for his sister, and through a wall.

"Don't lose him!" Josephine yelled, her eyes suddenly alert.

They started running, making their way around the building to the other side just as the boy walked out of the wall and down the street, heading towards the Christ Church cathedral and the old slave market.

Stone Town turned into a small village, the buildings melting away to the boy's glowing fists shining light on the huts around him. In the preternatural glow, the huts seemed to phase in and out of existence, growing wavy and blurry, becoming solid again only as the boy walked away.

Instead of the cathedral there was a house, rather large with wooden panels covering the windows, reddish brown paint flaking, revealing the brown stonework beneath it. The house vanished as he approached, and flashed back to existence as he walked up the small stairs.

Innocent followed him without hesitating, Josephine on her heels.

The house was dark, a long hallway dividing it in two with rooms on either side and a white tiled kitchen ending it, shining with the moonlight through the window. The walls of the hallway were painted a dark blue, bursting with light as the glow from the young boy's fists glided past them. When he walked by the doors they melted, revealing an empty bed on the left, and the boy's mother sleeping fitfully on the right across the hall.

The third room to the left was a small living room with a table and four chairs and a simple brown couch. An old radio set rested on the table and behind the table was a small wood and glass cupboard, filled with plates and glasses. The table was set for breakfast in the morning, a family of four that could have been happy, if not for the commotion, the sound of broken glass, and the screams coming from the last door by the kitchen.

The boy stood before the door, that remained solid despite his presence, the light gaining in strength, enveloping his whole body in its pink and blue hues.

He breathed deeply, his eyes wet with tears, staring at the door, breathing in the screams, his resolve growing by the second. "Don't worry Jen," he said. "Its almost over. I'm here now. He will never hurt you again."

A snarl appeared on his lips, then a grin, and he slammed a fist into the wooden door, that exploded inward, the screams stopped, and he stepped in.

Another scream rang in the night.

His own.

Josephine and Innocent ran towards the door, the scream turning to the bellows of denial.

"No! No no no no no no no!"

The young boy was on his knees in the room, cradling someone in his arms. A large naked man lied on the floor slumped against a small bed, his carcass bleeding from his throat, a piece of glass protruding from his neck, his eyes glazed, his face frozen in shock, his hands and arms still twitching.

And in the young boy's arms, his baby sister, half naked, her nightgown torn, her left wrist slit, artery coughing up thick bursts of blood, a piece of glass in her right hand.

She looked oddly vibrant under the pink blue light glowing from her brother, her eyes quiet and smiling, looking up at him with all the love she had left.

"What have you done Jen?" he asked, his voice shaking, the clatter of his teeth breaking the eerie silence. "Why did you do this?"

Jendyose inhaled, the blood flowing harder from her open veins.

"I couldn't take it anymore, James. I couldn't take it anymore. I'm sorry James, I'm sorry I've hurt you. I love you very much. He'll never harm me, or anyone again."

And with her last breath she was gone, her exhalation immaculate white like the shape of her soul melting into the blue pink glow, and disappeared.

James pounded her chest, shook her body and ran his fingers through her hair.

"I was too late," he said. "Too late. I was too late. Too late..."

The glow from his hands burst out of his body, floating over him, losing its colorful hues and turning blood red, slowly coagulating and turning into a thick black gob like a blood clot.

James looked up, suddenly remembering the mganga's words.

If you fail to stop the evil you will become the evil yourself...

The ball of black ooze stopped gyrating above him and dropped, drowning him, entering his mouth, ears and nostrils, slowly chocking him, his sister's body rolling out of his arms as he convulsed on the floor his body twisted on itself, and slowly started changing shape.

The house dissolved around them and Josephine and Innocent found themselves outside in Stone Town once again, the stained glass windows of the cathedral a thousand tiny glimmers of hope, and in front of them a tall black shape, with wings like bat, claws protruding from its shoulder blades, hands crooked like thorny stems, one single eye open in the middle of its face, crying blood tears over a face with no nose, but fanged like the fish that dwelled in the darkest depths, an erect penis the size of a large club, a cyclopean banshee, looming over a young man crawling away in mute terror.

It turned towards the sisters, who couldn't move, their eyes streaming with tears, looking inside their hearts for a trace of the faith that sustained them through the darkest times, but finding none.

"I was too late to save her," it said with a hiss, taking a step towards them, its wings wide open as if about to take flight. It lowered his sharp fingers, the black vertical slit in his red eye closing. "I couldn't save her." it said, its hand dropping, Josephine and Innocent lurching towards him.

"Stop!" Innocent screamed.

"Stop!" Josephine echoed. "There are many gods out there. One of them can still save your sou…"

They were too late. His clawed hand finished its sweep, slicing across his humongous cock, splattering Josephine and Innocent with its blood.

It dropped to its knees, clouds of black murder streaming from its body in the twisted shapes of his victims leaving only a skinny, naked young man, curly hair caked with filth, bleeding to death on the pavement, a smile on his lips.

EPILOGUE

"Sister Okala! Sister Lukyamuzi!"

Josephine and Innocent turned around. Night was falling slowly over Kampala, the smoke from thousands of small fires carrying the spicy smells of dinner, the courtyard of their school and orphanage slowly growing darker, and smiled at the young boy running up to them.

"What is it Dilman?" Innocent said.

The boy hesitated.

"It's my father," he said. He looked around making sure they were alone and whispered in their ears. "I think he is abusing my little brother."

At that very moment, a colony of bats flew over their heads, squeaking their way into the night. They both paused, remembering the young man who had loved so vibrantly, and lived and died so darkly, alone and in pain. How things had so easily returned to normal, as if nothing had happened, as if life and death and the thin dividing line between them was as meaningless as a jump rope.

It was good to be home again, but a part of them would always be in Stone Town, Zanzibar. The part of them that doubted. But their determination and faith?

Both had been restored, burning more brightly than ever.

They shuddered, then shook their heads, smiling at each other, and held Dilman close.

"Its OK." Josephine said. "You don't have to be afraid."

"No you don't." Innocent finished, "We'll take care of this. Personally."

BLACK
&
GOLD

(Routers) - Total is on the verge of signing an agreement for oil and gas exploration off Senegal's Atlantic coast, in a deal that could transform the country's agricultural economy.

Deep water Exploration will begin at the Rufisque Offshore Profond Block shortly after the deal is signed. Total as the main operator will hold a 90 percent stake and Senegal's state-run oil company Petrosen will hold the remaining 10 percent.

The exact financial terms of the deal were not disclosed.

"These agreements are part of the group's strategy to carry out exploration activities in new deep water basins in Africa." Total's chief executive Pascal Douyanne said in a statement.

Total currently owns 174 service stations but has no actual production in Senegal, the deal would fit within the company's objective of cheaper investments with the hope of greater returns.

Concerns have been expressed by environmental NGOs, Senegalese worker's unions and corruption watchdogs from various agencies.

"We are very concerned," says Mbissane Diouf of Anti-Corruption Senegal "If measures aren't taken in advance we will see a repeat of the disastrous environmental repercussions that have plagued Nigeria's Niger Delta in their deal with British Petroleum. Senegalese local fishermen are still reeling from deals made under the Wade administration granting fishing rights to Russian and major Western powers. Senegal is a small economy and the risks of Dutch Disease are incredibly high, Senegalese nationals will no longer be able to afford living in their own country. There are at this stage no signs of protection or favorable conditions for Senegalese workers. How will the country benefit if Total simply sends its own workers from France or imports cheaper labor from the rest of the sub region? And of course, there is word of backhand deals signed with local politicians and religious leaders to favor Total over the people. There is potential in this off shore exploration deal, great potential, but also all the signs of a potential calamity."

(Reporting by Svetlana Khanaeva in Paris and James McTavish in Dakar. Editing by Jennifer Malone and Donald Edwards)

He didn't dream anymore. He never truly slept anymore either. He didn't need to, but when he closed his eyes he would find himself in other whens, reliving his ancestors' lives, feeling their thoughts and the anticipation of the future that he sent back at them through time. And sometimes his dreams were his own, and every time the shining white horse found him, charging down at him on the beaches of Yoff Layene.

The drumbeats made their way through the sandy streets, through the smoke drifting from pyres, carrying the smell of grilled meats, the iodine of salty seas, the sharp scent of dead fish unloaded on the shores, and the smell of burning corpses. They covered the moans of the orgy that would only abate long enough for the guests to sleep a few hours before returning to their homes, to be replaced by more famished supplicants waiting to make their offerings to him, in whichever currency or valuables they had, and if not, their naked, lewd forms.

Khadim looked upon the sleeping shapes of the women lying naked in front of him, their chocolate brown skin shinny with the sweat of their exertion, tightly woven braids entangled like their legs in a knot of sensual abandon. They smelled of churaï and smoke, of desire and cum, of sand and hope.

He hadn't known that hope had a smell, but over the past few weeks, since he had started holding court, he had learned to recognize it. It was always the same, a tingle of anticipation, a smidgen of love and a dash of fear. It was those things that made up hope, the uncertainty of it.

How does one measure love? He didn't. You don't measure it but let it overwhelm you. If it overwhelmed him enough he granted them their wish. If it didn't? Well, he would ask them for a deed and send them on a mission.

"Rab?" one of the women said waking up, lifting her head from the breasts of another.

"Yes, loved one," he answered, looking ahead into the thin smoke to the timid rays of sunlight seeping through the low concrete buildings marked in cattle blood.

"Will my son be healed?"

"He already is, loved one."

"So I may return to my village?

"You always could, loved one, you never had to stay longer than you wished. Thank you for your offering."

She threw her arms around his pudgy neck, the sweat from her breasts imprinting his black and red shirt.

"Thank you Rab! Thank you so much."

He pushed her away gently. "Don't thank me," he answered. "Leuk Daour Mbaye looks after his own. Go back to your village, go back to your son, hold on to your hope, it is what makes you shine."

She backed away, her eyes wet with tears, careful not to tread on the others, and faded into the morning light.

She was pure. Others were not.

He turned to two young men tied to a poll on the far end of the tent, their eyes wide with lust and horror, smelling the burnt flesh of those who held no love but wanted his powers for themselves, for their own greedy passions.

"You," he said, "you who would sell your own kind given a chance. Will you do something for me? Will you redeem yourselves for your people?"

They nodded frantically.

"Wow, Rab!"

"Yes! Anything."

"Very good," he said approaching them, just as careful not to step over the sleeping bodies of the sex drunk revelers. He placed a hand on each of their foreheads. "Look deep into your minds. This is whom you must kill. If you don't, I will know. I will find you. Bring me back their heads."

———

(Routers) – No one can explain what is happening in Senegal yet.

French tourists having travelled to the country in the past three weeks are still unaccounted for, and the crowds gathering outside the Elysée presidential palace in Paris are not leaving, despite the pressure from local police.

Among the missing, is Routers' very own James McTavish, our permanent correspondent in Dakar.

Planes flying to the country suddenly disappear from the radar as they enter Senegalese airspace. It is unclear whether they have landed or crashed, or if something else is happening entirely.

"On ne sait vraiment pas quoi leur dire. It's baffling but none of the planes have returned and we cannot reach anyone in the country. It's as if Senegal has gone off the grid. The entire country," says Presidential spokesperson, Michel Devedjian. "We are doing the best we can."

All flights to the West African nation have been cancelled. French president Nathalie Mauroir is calling an international conference to address the issue.

(Reporting by Svetlana Khanaeva in Paris. Editing by Jennifer Malone and Donald Edwards)

The streets of Plateau district should have been filled with cars, street vendors, people in blue work shirts haggling with cab drivers, grandmothers in colorful headdresses, and children racing through traffic, small rice bowls in their tiny hands begging for food and coin, and laughing and fighting among each other. The vehicles left abandoned haphazardly as in the aftermath of a neutron bomb spoke of their absence in more ways than crowded streets could have. The throngs of people in a file marching to his beat behind him filled the air with the sweaty fragrance of life.

He'd been one of those children once, his parents too poor to send him anywhere but to the madrassa. The early mornings had been his favorite part. The hustle and bustle of downtown Dakar in the cool breeze coming in from the cliffs, only a few hours before the heat dropped like a wooly blanket over them. People were different in the morning, he'd noticed. Some were still sleepy and irritable but there was an electric tingle to it all, the new day fueling hope with sunrays that washed away the drowsiness. His chubby self hardly kept up with the other kids, yet determined to beg a meal for himself. For an hour or so they were all in the same boat, the camaraderie of poverty, and the equal inequality of childhood.

That feeling never lasted, neither did the fact, eventually the other kids would shove him to the ground and steal whatever coin he had hustled, eat whatever food he had gleaned claiming his fat ass had enough to feed on for days and they should probably feed on him. He didn't sleep many a night imagining them coming down on him, clawing his flesh apart with their bare hands as he wasn't allowed to die, feeling not only the pain, but their young hatred, that just as a child's love poured unfiltered and raw.

He turned to look back at the procession.

The torches of his followers trailed out of sight behind him, twisting and turning in the twilight like a snake of flame, chanting traditional verses that he'd heard on weekends home with his family in Marché Yoff.

The women's voices rang louder than the others, high pitched notes that hung in the air and dropped like shooting stars, echoing down the side streets, and catching up with the procession around the next corner, praising him and his return to save Dakar, to save them all.

Yoff had been a different place, removed from the Plateau's accelerated modernity that was torn out of the city's soul reflecting an ideal that wasn't its own. Yoff shared in the scars, the foreign banks and bakeries, the supermarkets and gas stations. But as he walked away from the expressway, down streets that grew slimmer, increasingly covered in sand and lined with traditional stores, he moved back into Africa, small family houses with crowded courtyards full of poultry and goats, and the smell of mint tea and weed, of grilled lamb and beef skewers, of dried fish.

Going home had been a relief, but only temporary, hoping against hope that he would find there the love he lacked at the madrassa, but his family never extended it to him.

It was odd how his memories floated to the surface sometimes, now that he could look through every building and see its bones, look down at the concrete and see the old terrain beneath, look at his followers and read each of their souls, look into the distance and focus his eyes on events hundreds of miles away. He was still Khadim somewhere deep, and while his new powers thrilled him, he found comfort in being the young boy he always had been, who had known he would grow to bigger things.

They walked by the old presidential palace, white stones polished and arranged to mimic a culture that had sought to erase their own, still burning somewhere deep. The metal gates hung from their frame, torn open, and on the two spikes that boarded them, the president and the prime minister's heads stared into the distance, spikes rising from their skulls through their necks, hollow eye sockets picked away by birds in a vacant state that reflected their vacant lives. Their skin had started to rot away, lips rolled up in menacing snarls. Their time had come, his people had done well. They threw stones at the heads when they walked by.

Those people who had abused their trust, sold their land's blood, and drank of it.

When he wandered the beach as a child, in the cover of darkness wishing no one would see him and notice his flabby skin and his lazy eye, dreaming of bigger things, of a day when they would all see how beautiful he was, the white horse would follow him. It walked up to him, seven feet high at the shoulders, its beige mane flowing down its neck like a sand dune blowing away in the wind, nuzzling him, pushing him forward and never letting him rest.

He would pat it and speak to it softly. When he told the others about it they laughed. No one saw it but him.

The procession made it to the cliffs lining the coast, the rocky brown surfaces singing with the beating of the waves and the last rays of the setting sun bouncing off the oil rigs dotting the horizon, black and grey sleek skeletons of carrion birds, feeding and feeding and feeding some more.

He knelt down closing his eyes, and applied his palm to the ground, feeling through it. The multiple layers of soil, of rock, pockets of air forming caves larger than countries, the powdered bones of old things resting in the darkness, the heat that grew until it became liquid stone, and ripping through it all like teeth through charred meat, the mechanical pump of the machines cordoning off the ocean like prison bars.

He opened his eyes.

A crack resounded from the cliffs, raining boulders into the ocean, and the tiniest of waves grew, foaming at the edges, drawing more water in its wake, speeding towards the rigs like a shark's fin. It stretched from one cliff to the other then one horizon to the other, thundering like a thousand stampeding hooves, crashing into the rigs, ripping flame across itself like the breath of the earth, and vanished, leaving only a black cloud of smoke that melted in the clouds, and the prison bars were gone.

He rose, looking at the last of the rigs collapsing into the water.

The crowd cheered and wept with joy, and they marched on.

She'd had a sleepless night. The kind you get when you actually sleep but your dreams are so lucid they become a reality.

In her dream she was at sea. Rowing on one of the fishing boats her brother and cousins took off on for days, bringing back fish, shells and sometimes, adolescent hammerhead sharks.

Everybody revered them, and now she was one of them, the first and only woman ever allowed the honor. The sea reflected the sun in glaring streaks, painting the cerulean golden and silver, the bubbly foam riding like kori shells.

She breathed in the deep iodine, noticing that something was missing from it. It was her first time out and her heightened senses registered everything.

The air was pure, almost too pure.

"What are you sniffing for, Coumba?" her brother asked, laughing as her head darted about trying to understand what was missing from the smell. "This is not a hunt baby sister, and you are not a hyena."

Images of the forest flashed through her mind as he said that. She saw trees, she smelled mangrove rising from the riverbanks beyond it, the fresh fruit growing on the trees in abundance falling to the dirt road and shattering on the ground. So many of them there was no point picking them up. Fallen fruit were for animals that couldn't pick their own, not for people... And it hit her. She smelled the sea for the first time, and only the sea, unadulterated by the smell of land and human filth. Just the sea, pure and clean and alive.

There was a gust of wind, the clouds darkened at once, and the sky rumbled.

"Oh no," Famera, one of the other fishing boys said looking up, "it's gonna be a bad one."

The waves picked up on cue with the wind. When one moment the sea was placid, the next it rocked the boat like a boiling pot, sending it flying up and smashing down like a seesaw.

Coumba's shoulder crashed into one of the benches, deep bellows of thunder marking the storm's tempo. Her brother leaped towards her shaking her frantically.

"Wake up Combo! Wake up! We have to run! Now!"

Wake up? She thought drowsily, *Run? But there is nowhere to...*

The thunder turned to gunshots as her eyes popped open, Lamine standing in front of her still shaking her, blood streaming from an open cut in his forehead.

"Wake up little sister, they're coming for us!"

The smell of burning thatch tickled her nose and stung her eyes, the walls of their small hut shaking with the gun blasts that rung her ears as she scrambled to her feet, still dizzy with sleep, her vision split between her village and the marauding ocean.

She rushed out. Half the huts in the village consumed in flames, Lamine dragging her by the arm, making his way through the acrid smoke.

"Follow me! We gotta make it to the mangrove! They won't find us ther…"

A bullet finished his sentence for him, and he fell flat on his face, his skull breaking with a crack that seemed to drown the pandemonium around her in the moonless night of bonfires.

A heavy weight dropped on her back, pinning her to the ground. She thought it was a dead body, and started to scream, but a blood stained hand covered her mouth. She bit into the fingers, but they wouldn't let go, instead another pair of hands gripped her wrists tying them together with a sharp liana cutting into her skinny forearms.

She kicked but more lianas tied her ankles together, and she was pulled through the dirt by her hair.

She could barely look up, but noticed her assailants' dark skin, the heavy shoulders dragging her forward, and the bracelets that they wore. She knew that pattern. The carvings on the silver told her they were from a neighboring village a little ways north of them along the coast.

But why? She thought, as her captor made his way more slowly through the sand leading to the beach, the wind blowing mockingly into her face.

"Why? Why are you doing this!" she asked the liana growing tighter with every movement.

The roots of her hair stung like flames searing the top of her scalp. Every bit of sand as gritty and abrasive as rusty copper as she was dragged into the darkness away from the flames of her village, the silence of her ravishers a disconnect that she barely endured. Worse yet than their actions, a denial of her existence that made her feel like the small game she had learned to stone with a slingshot as a child. Lamine had refused to let her grow unable to fend for herself despite her father repeating that a good woman would find a good man to do these things for her. She had asked him what a good woman meant, and had been slapped for it.

The darkness and screams gave way to the soothing sound of waves licking the beaches in hypnotic carnal desire, and the gleaming of stars torn by milky clouds, and in the distance, on the waters of her dream, lights. Lights in horizontal symmetry floating eerily over the waters and an oblong shadow, pointed at its ends with ghostly sheets of white catching the stars and the lights beneath it invitingly.

She had heard of such shapes, she had been told of such ships, where screams drowned and bodies vanished.

She struggled against all hope, her skinny shape pounded repeatedly into immobility in the same inhuman silence that she dreaded.

There was nowhere to go, no one to help.

Her brain raced, wondering what had driven the villagers to do such a thing. Who had given them those weapons? Didn't they know that the same people who used them to hurt her would use others to hurt them in turn?

She was young, but few things make a young mind wiser than the absurdity of greed in the face of pain.

She wanted to scream, she wanted to beg, she wanted the sacred wood to turn into a giant and tear off their heads. But it didn't and neither did she. She had been raised to be proud, in spite of everything. To be proud, and in the deadly silence of horny waves she heard hooves on the beach near her, the deep breathing of a beast, and its musky smell.

She turned her head against the scarring sand.

There it stood, gleaming in the starlight, white coat split by a mane the color of pure sand, standing taller at the shoulders than any but the tallest men, smoke blowing out of its nostrils, staring into her eyes with auburn brown compassion.

She yelled then, called into it, to come crush her captors and pound their pulped organs into the sand, but her own thunder never left her lungs, soothed into silence by the beautiful beast on the beach.

Her captors showed no signs of seeing it, but the anger on their faces faded under the animal's hypnotic stare, as she was drawn out of her body into another now.

It wasn't hers to see. Coumba knew she wasn't really part of the scene, only an unwitting witness caught in the chaos of confusion.

The sun was the same; the waves and sea were the same as in her dream; only the smell had changed. It was thick. It lingered on the tongue oily and wrong. The smell of something never meant to be, of a million years dead.

She was the wind and the flow of the waves, she was the seagull trying to get away, and the shark deep beneath that had ignored the currents and been caught in the whirlpool. She was everything that was nature, and everything that abhorred her surroundings.

Structures burst out of the waves, slick grey structures with a quality not of her world, dug into the depths where her family fished, having killed all their prey. She felt the anger of the earth and the anger of the soil. These were greedy beasts.

She had heard that somewhere in the stars there were people. Perhaps the things were of their making. Anchored in the depths, stretching to the clouds bleeding black blood, and puffing fires into the sky. So alien yet so human.

And yet they burned.

Their perfection was marred. Collapsing like her village was.

The white skinned men that had all the weapons held none, diving off sleek platforms into the uninviting waters rather than feel their flesh dissolve like tallow and float off in the wind.

She felt their pain. They were not guilty, but they couldn't have been there then if she wasn't here now, dragged by her hair on a beach that she thought she had known but didn't help her. Connected now, connected back, connected forward. Past, present and future; all different and yet the same.

She caught a glimpse of a distant riff, felt the beating of a past drum roll, and she smiled, watching the towers collapse into the sea, and knowing her part in things.

The vision faded. The pain returned.

Her skin burning from the wooden planks incrusted with dry salt cutting into it.

She screamed as she was thrown down the wooden stairs into an abyss of rotten feces and unwashed flesh, screamed as she was shackled to a plank that she may never survive, but she smiled when the rocking of the waves picked up, smiled knowing that somewhere, deep into the future there was hope.

———

Khadim awoke screaming, the mouth of the foreign woman wrapped around his cock biting him in sheer panic. His nose reeled with the smell of dried shit, his eyes blinded by the lights of a wooden vessel cutting through the waves into the night. He came with the pain, and fell back asleep.

———

(Routers) – The inexplicable situation in Senegal worsens.

As previously reported a wave of disappearances of airplanes, passengers and airline personnel in Senegal, has sent France and its citizens into disarray.

Weeks of public protests have turned downtown Paris into a small city within the city, as makeshifts tents, trailers and even sheet metal houses, have flourished, hosting people coming in from all parts of the country demanding explanations from the Elysée presidential palace, only a few blocks from the Champs Elysees. Paris' most popular tourist destination and home to high end shopping venues and restaurants now a sprawling shantytown.

Major public events such as the upcoming Tour de France have been cancelled, as well as popular celebrations such as La Fête de la Musique.

Helicopters, which are not usually allowed to fly over the city, are constantly surveilling the downtown encampments as well as regular patrols of CRS, France's riot police, although more for the purposes of ensuring public safety than repression this time around.

"Je veux savoir ou sont ma femme et mes enfants. It's crazy! They have been missing for weeks and no one can tell me anything. My wife and kids! What would you do if it were yours? The government owes us an explanation, why aren't they doing something?" Asks Ahmed Douraidi, a disgruntled father of two.

The phenomenon is not limited to France. Germany, Nigeria, China and the United States have also reported missing airplanes and an absolute lack of communication with the West African nation.

Total disappearances have risen to 1293 so far, as in addition to the missing plane passengers; foreign citizens having travelled earlier to the country are also being tallied.

"It is time to take matters in our own hands." German Chancellor Susanne Melde announced at a press conference early Tuesday morning. "We have sat to talk about the ongoing situation in Senegal with President Mauroir of France. The country is preparing to deploy Rafale fighter jets towards Senegal. While it is not a preferred solution, we are hopeful that the Senegalese government will see reason and respond to the pressing matters at hand."

(Reporting by Svetlana Khanaeva in Paris. Editing by Jennifer Malone and Donald Edwards)

There was something about the clouds. How their streaming past him made him feel like Santa Claus. Flying through them he recaptured his childhood. The clouds were ghosts, the clouds were streams of immortality. He had looked at the clouds as a little boy and thought: *this is me.*

Nothing is the same when you're a child. Everything is a dream, but you're told to dream...

So Arnaud had failed as a student, but as pilot...Well...damn...

Rudolf's red nose was the tip of his fighter jet. It wasn't gifts that he dropped from the sky. It was rockets and payloads, but there was a purpose, a reality that said: guy, be all you can be, be everything you dreamed, just be, just be, because there is very little else beyond your dream.

He blasted out of Paris at Mach 2.2, the ground beneath a blur of green grass and mountains long shriveled, and people, dotting the land like pawns in a chess game.

The lands of Oï turned to sea, open waters of sapphire calm, of foam over waves that beat with the absence of a heart like his own, like the child he'd been, loaded with gifts, and then it was gone.

It was gone but never stopped, blurring back into green, replaced in a beat with the brownish gold of the dunes. Dunes that never ended, dunes that a thousand years prior were wet valleys and had changed.

The dunes never ended, they flowed like the humps on the back of a camel disappearing in a flash just as his target registered on his radar.

And then...

Je me souviens de cette fille...

Good god he remembered this girl. He remembered her as if he knew her.

He stood on a boat caught between a sea that could kill him and a continent that could make him rich.

She had been dragged through the sand, dragged ignorant of what she would become to suffer a promise that wasn't her own.

He wept.

Arnaud hadn't wept since he was nine. When he had opened his head against a window playing soccer with his brothers. He had found fifty francs on his way out and his pain had abated some. But not this pain, this pain he could only witness helplessly.

He looked down from a cloudless sky. Someone in Louisiana carrying his name, putting out the light on his torch, walking into the barn, carrying a noose menacingly as the young girl of the boat crawled away into a corner, after having already lived through so much...

Arnaud lifted his helmet in midflight, and spoke into the radio.

"Enough." He said, "Enough. I am landing."

Khadim wandered the beach, famished.

The pungent mix of wet plastic bags and soggy cardboard boxes, leftover stinking carcasses of crabs, lobster and jellyfish, speckled with horse manure, smelt to him like the most fantastic meal he had never had. As if he could taste the feast of seafood others were having across the ocean, the delighted chews of fresh grass the horses had enjoyed unaware of better things.

His young mouth watered at the sight of them, just as his stomach threatened to turn into a black hole and eat him alive from the inside, growling with the lament of a dying beast.

For three days his madrassa companions had beaten him out of the little money he had begged for, leaving him to lick the little drips of sauce and half chewed leftover grains of rice they had been too careless to have. Filling himself with water had worked at first, but his empty stomach, gorged with acid, rejected every sip the way it came in, leaving him in fits of bile, his throat burning and his eyes dazed and red with fatigue.

His family had denied him the family bowl to eat with his brothers, giving him a lashing for failing to bring back any coin from his week begging on the Plateau.

He hadn't showered in days, and the few people walking the beach in the evening stepped away from him, pinching their noses and shaking their fingers at him, muttering fowler words than his young mind could comprehend.

He fiddled with the small knife in his pocket, tempted to carve out a chunk of his own flesh, as his little comrades had taunted him to do. What did he have to lose? If he asked any of the neighbors for subsistence they would thrash him and send him home for another thrashing. Perhaps he tasted better than he gave himself credit for.

The familiar sound of hooves didn't register. Lost in thought Khadim took out his knife and sat on the beach, right where the waves ate the sand with softness and applied the blade to his forearm.

"Lala Illah la, la la Illah la," he repeated trembling, hesitating between cutting his veins or waiting for the tide to wash him away.

Drops of drool hit his shoulder, the warm nudge of the horse's muzzle lowered into his neck, trying to comfort his infant loneliness.

Perhaps if he had been older he would have known better and thought twice. Perhaps if he had been more accustomed to hunger, the smell of flesh wouldn't have assailed his nostrils and aroused his stomach. But he was young. He was hungry. He was alone. Alone in a world full of people.

He spun and slammed his knife into the white horse's neck, gluing his lips to the geyser of blood pouring out, slurping and drinking all that he could, the thick syrup layering his stomach, coating it with life.

His knife dug in some more, carving chunks of hairy flesh out of the falling beast.

He chewed through them. Attacked its stomach, its liver, and its ribs. He ate and ate. Ate volumes his small body couldn't handle and when all the flesh was gone nibbled the tendons off the bones, reached for the spine and cracked it open, sucking the marrow till it was dry, crushing its skull to suck out its brain, quenching his first into the poisonous waters of the sea.

He turned on to his slaughter, his needs satiated, his soul bursting through his pores, exploding with life, exploding with love.

He realized then that he had never known love, only the longing for it, and fell back on the beach, his head resting on the immaculate white bones like a pillow.

And he dreamed.

A turbaned warrior on a white horse, meeting a gathering of chiefs under broad tents and an open arena. A call to arms and a call for blood. A battle between swords and horses and white men in blue uniforms screaming death from metal sticks that took the horses and the warriors alike.

He led the charge, racing into the banging death, uncaring of his fate, uncaring of his pain, knowing only that he had only now, only then...

"Rab." a voice resounded through the fog. "Rab…"

Kneeling in front of him were two men, garbed in the camou-flaged green of fighter pilots, looking up at him tears running from their eyes down their cheeks and hitting the ground with the strength of monsoon, an echo of thunderclaps with the softness of dew.

Two women held them by strings tied around their wrists behind their backs.

"Rab." one asked. "What shall we do with them?"

He looked into their eyes, and saw the young boy who had fallen asleep, his belly full, his heart content, who had grown everyday stronger, everyday more aware, everyday more powerful until the man who sat before them was here, decades later, when the need had called upon him.

"What shall you do with them? Nothing. Free them, and treat them well. They have learned their part in things. They have earned their place."

The Baye Fall spun in dervish frenzy. Dreadlocks and multicolored garbs creating small singularities, blurred and warped in the middle of the smoke and flames while Leuk Daour's followers dragged men and women through the sand from the tent, tying their crying bodies caked with sand and dread-filled sweat to posts, dousing them in raw gasoline and setting them on fire.

"La illah! La illalah! La Illahaaah! La illalah!!"

The festive singing belied the chained prisoners' wails. Outside of Khadim's red and black tent rising over the buildings like a small hill the bonfires raged fiercer than they had in weeks.

"Bitte!"

"La Illah!"

"Mo be e!"

"La Illalah!"

"Wǒ qiú qiú nǐ!"

"La Illahaaah! La Illalah…"

The smoke should have burned the singers' lungs but under Leuk Daour's protection the oil's poison faded into the air, leaving only the odor of wood and flesh to find its way over and around the city in the night.

Sitting on his gilded chair inside the tent, Khadim looked at the line of foreigners and faithful waiting for his judgement; their eyes open in wonder, the others incredulous at where they were and what they witnessed.

Do they see me as I see myself? He wondered.

He knew it didn't matter, whatever they saw was blinded by the strength of the spirit inside him. By his purpose. He had often heard that great people projected who they were inside despite what they were. A tiny man with the ambitions of a lion appeared as a lion to others. Larger, stronger, his energy cloaking him like thunder. An ugly woman who knew her worth was more attractive than a beautiful one with a shallow mind. Perhaps he appeared as a seven-foot wrestler, perhaps as a marauding elephant, perhaps as a silverback gorilla.

Next to him, the griot recited his family line. His voice rhythmical and hypnotic, praising his great-great-great-grandfather who, rumor had it, had held a battalion of French soldiers at bay alone for three days when they had come muskets in hand to claim his land to build a railroad to Bamako. Sang of his great grandmother's beauty, so beautiful she had suitors from Dahomey to Nouakchott and had chosen a low cast blacksmith over chiefs and their sons.

They were all lies. He had come from nothing. Only someone who was truly nothing could ever become something, unencumbered by the weight of expectations, by the doubt that grew from following greatness and having to fill bigger shoes than your small feet could handle.

"Leuk Daour Mbaye! Rab Leuk Daour Mbaye, made flesh once again to protect Dakar! Allah's blessings onto you! Leuk Daour Mbaye is here. You have nothing to fear."

There was some truth there. The truth of his purpose.

"Rab," a young man said leaning over, a gun pointed at a group of British tourists. "Where shall I burn them?"

Khadim looked at the shivering people. Their children held

closely to them, peering into their hearts. They were like him, sons and daughters of coal miners, an orphan who had lost his parents in the Great War. Children too young to know better.

"Fool," he said "you are too quick to judge. Let them go and leave with them. Let them walk free until their fine clothes have worn off and you see yourself in them. Until they see themselves in you. Until you have both lost the pretention of your station and are as your mother's had dreamt you."

The families threw themselves at his feet.

"Thank you sir!" a mother said "For the sake of our children, thank you."

He cupped her chin and stared her in the eye. "You will leave your children with me," he said. "When you return, they will be here waiting, to teach you a new way."

She began to weep, and he tore a piece of his shirt to wipe her tears. "They will be cared for, you have my word. Now go, and find yourselves."

Her husband knelt behind her and nodded, pulling her up by the shoulders. "We will come back for them," he said.

Khadim nodded and laughed. "I hope you do. This is the time for the children to lead, for the former slaves to run the fields. Now go."

Two women came forth, naked at the waist, wearing beads around their necks and bracelets on their arms.

They took the children by the hand. They didn't cry, only stared at their parents compassionately, and waved them goodbye.

Khadim sighed. "Who is next?" he asked.

Two young men came forth, carrying bloody bur sacks in their hands, the droplets of blood swallowed by the sand at their feet.

"Rab," one said. "We have done what you have asked. We have brought you their heads."

They opened the sacks and let the two skulls roll at his feet.

"Who were they, Rab?"

He looked down. He had never met the men but had seen them in a vision. One had abused his authority as a man of God, and cheated poor villagers out of their land for the sake of the other, who had come to build a highway he would never finish, had stolen a young girl's honor with fake promises and words of love.

One was an imam and one was a contractor. One was black and one was white. Both were guilty.

"They were who you were," he said. "They did what you would have done."

The two boys looked at each other.

"But we have done well, Rab."

"We have done what you asked."

"You have. And for that you will live. But never come back."

They backed away exiting the tent. He had no doubt they were still greedy at heart, but knew they would never fulfill it now, that every step of their life they would look over their shoulders, feeling his gaze burning the nape of their necks.

"… Leuk Daour Mbaye is here. You have nothing to fear."

(Routers) – It is all so clear now.

It should have been before. As a professional I apologize.

The crowds around the Elysée have melted.

The government's chitter chatter has faded, and we as journalists have lost our purpose.

The gone are never coming back. The lost have found a new home.

If we had only been smarter we would have connected the dots. The disappearances began only a few weeks after the exploration deal with Total was signed. Despite continued reassurances by Total CEO, Pascal Douyanne, Senegalese national petroleum company Petrosen would have only started profiting from the deal after 20 years and only 10% of annual profits.

Total also reneged on its promise to maintain a 50% Senegalese labor force in all activities including local managerial positions, flying in workers directly from France at a premium to be born almost exclusively by Petrosen and deducted from delayed profits.

The first disappearances were the planes carrying Total employees.

How any of this possible and what is happening on the ground remains a mystery, but we cannot ignore the timing, French President Mauroir's administration, including herself, have resigned and a month of mourning has been announced in France, Germany, Britain, the United States of America, Nigeria, Niger, China and Bangladesh. Other countries are deploring the absence of their citizens.

Senegal has gone completely off the grid; no communications have come out of the country since the incidents were first reported. Satellite surveillance reportedly blurs when attempts are made to surveille the ground.

Routers will be joining in the month long mourning ceremonies.

Our thoughts and prayers are with the missing and the people of Senegal.

(Reporting by Svetlana Khanaeva in Paris. Editing by Jennifer Malone and Donald Edwards)

He doesn't dream anymore. He never truly sleeps anymore either. Even wide-awake his breaths are haunted by crippling visions of a future he can no longer control. Of all that he had wrestled against coming forth ten, a hundred fold. Other whens filled with pain and loathing, and the curse that has become his name. In his darkest moments, when the stormy night sky meets a barren land and a sea filled with the floating carcasses of millions of fish, they find him. Their eyes red, the pounding of his hooves disappearing under their screams, and they attack him all at once, tearing out his flesh the way he had as a young boy, but they don't consume him, they leave him on the beach to rot without rebirth.

Khadim couldn't hear the moans. He couldn't smell the pyres. He couldn't see the tent.

The orgy spread outside of his palace, which is what his tent had become. Perhaps it's what it had always been and he had deluded himself.

The supplicants didn't fear the burning and the screams anymore, tearing each other's clothes off for all to see, fueled by the pain of the sacrifices around them. The dying souls fused with their own in a frenzy of lustful release. Bodies of all shapes and colors mingled together like the knotty roots of the baobab tree, bulging and reeving like a den of tangled snakes, slithering over each other for more flesh to bite, to swallow, to sink into.

He tried to focus his sight on them, but flashes of hyper heated sand turned to glass, reflecting a hungry sun blinded him everywhere he looked. Tremors shook the ground under his feet and throne, the sky a still blue, calm and uncaring looking down at a world he did not know. The smell on the humid monsoon breeze reeking of decaying flesh, filled with pain, anger, and resentment.

The tremors rocked him, rattling his bones inside his chest, threatening to break and tear through his heart.

"Rab!" a voice peered through the rumble "Rab! Wake up!"

His vision focused suddenly. The bombed out desert vanished. The lush and sweaty skin of one of his fanatics rolled in front of him, breasts pointing towards the roof of his tent, covered in a flash by a mouth and a mass of blond hair.

He looked into the empty eyes of one of his lieutenants. Fallou was it? Or maybe Samba?

It didn't matter. Fallou, Samba, or any one of the millions of fanatics, all had the same vacant look of adoration when they saw him. Empty, sheepish, ready to fuck, or kill or throw themselves into the fires at his will. Slaves. His slaves. They had become everything he had fought against; he had freed them for a time, broken past bonds and in doing so, had bonded them to him with the absent-mindedness of blind faith.

Khadim Mbaye the lonely child from Yoff Layene had become Leuk Daour Mbaye, the protective spirit of Dakar made flesh, and Leuk Daour Mbaye had become God.

"Rab!" the man said, "We have word of the border regions."

Khadim breathed in, soaking in the sound and smells, letting the heat draw sweat from his brow. The only few things that reminded him that somewhere, buried under the folds of fat and the fake comfort of adoration, there was still a man.

"Speak."

"People are trying to flee Rab. The crops haven't grown this year and there is no grain left to feed them. Wells are running dry as well. We are fixing the pipes, bringing in trucks from the city, but they still flee, Rab. We have calmed some, but too many are angry, Rab. They are cursing you. Blasphemy, Rab. Blasphemy."

The glassy black sand reappeared beneath his feet, the tremors shook. He breathed in and forced them away.

"So what have you done?"

"To the blasphemers?" he asked, a rare look of surprise, flashing through his eyes. "We set them on fire, Rab, all of them. It should have calmed the others but it only made them angrier. They charged at us Rab. So we shot them."

"All of them?" he asked remaining calm.

The young man nodded, a smile spreading across his lips with pride. "Yes, Rab! All of them!"

"The children too?"

"Yes Rab. Well, not all the children, some ran away but their parents are dead, Rab. They will not tarnish your name."

"How many?"

"I am not sure Rab. Two thousand people many more."

Khadim remained silent.

"We have done well. Haven't we Rab?" Fallou asked, the same look of pride on his face.

"You have done what you thought was right, Fallou." He said, feeling his power seep out of him. "And for that I must take the blame."

"I don't understand. You are not to blame Rab. You are Leuk Daour, the white horse, our protector and savior."

Khadim waved an exhausted arm at him.

"There is nothing to understand Fallou. Nothing to blame yourself for. Go join the others outside, you have earned your rest."

Fallou bowed his head, and walked backwards through the sea of bodies, and exited the tent.

...And their children, their hungry and thirsty children...

The sand turned to glass again beneath him, the tremor shook through his system, but he didn't push them away. He no longer had the strength, he no longer had the courage.

"Father?" the young boy asked.

In the darkness his raspy, halting breaths would have confused him for an older man, but in the clearing sunlight, his short stature and skinny frame left no doubt that, tough as he wanted to seem, there was a hopelessly sick young boy, struggling with every step.

His father turned back for the twentieth time that morning. It was so easy to get ahead of him and forget that he couldn't keep pace. The jagged terrain of what used to be desert sand gleaming of emerald and obsidian, layers upon layers of slagged silica appearing as if walking on a sea of congealed water, sometimes smooth slippery, sometimes cut and sharp as a razors edge.

"Yes, Dam."

"How much further to the Oasis?"

"Almost there son. A few hours at most."

But did Dam have a few hours? Water. Water was the only thing that kept the radiation sickness at bay. Water and a father's love. A dying child's unbreakable belief that his father would find a way.

Thierno slowed down, letting Dam catch up with him.

Reaching the Oasis was only the first step, the haggling would be next and all he had to negotiate with he carried on his back, his indigence plain for the world to see. He'd heard of people who left their sick children and family with the Man of the Oasis. Left them there to die with others like themselves and took the water away.

There was sense to that. Why waste time on a dying cause? Why not give them the mercy of a quick death rather than false hope and pain eating at their insides till they collapsed, all of their organs liquefied?

Thierno shook his head. He wouldn't do that to Dam. He wiped the sweat of the boy's brow, kneeled and let him climb on his back, carrying him the rest of the way.

The walls surrounding the Oasis loomed in the distance. Grey, concrete slabs pockmarked with bullet holes and darker patches where blood had long dried but never been cleaned. And inside... well he had only heard rumors of what was inside, but he had been told that paradise lay inside the walls, a land and city lush and plump with water. He couldn't quite imagine it, but he needed to believe.

As they approached the walls rising behind and over a hill, the glassy sand grew littered with discarded things. Clothes and cloths, cans and plastic, leather bags and bones. Thousands of bones, gleaming in the early afternoon sun. Skulls, femurs, cracked rib cages. So many bones.

The wall loomed higher than anything Thierno had ever seen; covered in markings and prayers, and in thick black letters a warning: "Fear, stranger, fear. Do not take another step, for Leuk Daour lives here."

Thierno shuddered. He held Dam tighter, but his attention was diverted by moans of pain and tears. Sitting along the dull grey façade thousands of people looked up in the sky, into the distance, emaciated to the point where they could make their way inside through the cracks in the concrete. He had been told about them too. Those who had been turned away, too tired to make their way home, too disillusioned to care, waiting patiently to join the bones around them.

Surprisingly the road leading to the massive metal doors barring entrance into the city was empty. Its sides lined with fresh corpses. As he approached, the two burly guards, dull eyed and carrying heavy machine guns opened the gates for him and made way.

"Thierno Sankara," they said in unison. "The Rab has told us you were coming."

Thierno simply nodded and went through, too tired, astounded and terrified to speak a word.

What is this place? He thought. *Where have I taken my son?*

His fears dissipated the moment he walked passed the gates. The glassy sand gave way to grass and thick baobab trees, flowers and the strong smell of the ocean beyond the buildings that stretched north and south beyond his vision. The fertile radiance almost blinded him, when a voice rang through his ears.

Come to the ocean, Thierno Sankara.

He walked. Dam asleep on his back, and marveled at the sights around him. He had heard that such cities had existed, but he didn't think he would have ever seen one. For all he knew there was no world outside of San'gaal, only a misty cloud that ate away at your flesh. Nothing beyond the lifeless expanses of the shattered landscape. Yet here he was. In the heart of the city. Finally inside the Oasis.

"Where are we father?" Dan's voice chimed behind him. "Are we there?"

He knew his son was too weak to open his eyes. "Almost, son. Almost. Be strong, only a moment longer."

"Yes, father."

They broke through a string of small houses covered in vines and thorns and onto an open square. Thierno had been so caught up in the sights he hadn't realized how silent the streets were, so empty of life. There were no people, no birds, no dogs, no insects, nothing. Life rung like a bell by its absence.

A large red and black tent stood in the middle of the square.

Come in Thierno Sankara, the voice echoed through his mind, *Come in.*

He felt a searing flash of doubt, his chest pressing coldly against his heart, every muscle in his body turning to mush, but he pushed his way through the flaps and into the tent.

It was empty and dark. The lingering smell of burnt flesh and sweat seeping from the very ground itself. In the center of it, on an old leather seat, sat the fattest man he had ever seen, his stomach flowing over the sides of his chair, his legs too thick and heavy to move, chin after chin rolling from his face over his belly, and his flabby arms holding what looked like a torn and bloody limb.

This can't be. Thierno thought. *This can't...be....*

The man looked up, his mouth covered in blood, one eye clear and intent, the other lazy and half closed.

He looked at Thierno, carrying his dying son on his back and said, "I see true love in you, Thierno Sankara. Truer love than I have seen in years. Come to me. Offer yourself and your son to your God."

No! Thierno thought, *No no no this is not what I've been told this is...*

But even as he thought this, his legs moved compulsively forward, even as he tried to turn away and run, run and save Dam, even if it killed him.

He couldn't turn, he could only move forward, closer to the enormous man flowing out of his chair and to the floor, dropping the bloody limb he held in his hand, a smile of pure kindness on his face and opening his arms, ready to crush him and his boy with them, and feed on their souls...

———

Khadim awoke, the taste of blood in his mouth, feeling Thierno's fear and care for his son filling his stomach, and vomited.

The swingers in the tent interrupted their lovemaking and stared at him in panic.

"Out!" he screamed, his voice a brontide rumble of grinding rocks in a storm "Out! All of you!"

His scream carried through Yoff, through Ngor and Ouakam, through Parcelles Assainies and Gueules Tapées, giving way to a stampede, to the pounding of feet hitting the ground furiously to the screams and broken bones of those trampled in the tumult, the panicked bleating of cattle and the screeches of birds and to sudden silence.

The eerie silence of his vision.

Is this what I become? Is this how it begins?

No.

No.

I will not let that happen.

He pushed himself slowly off his chair, buckling under his own weight. He hadn't stood up in weeks, feasting and fucking without feeling the earthly need to relieve himself he had grown larger than he ever thought he would.

But I can still walk, he thought, *I am not him yet.*

He stepped out of the tent, seeing for the first time the extent of the carnage he had ordered, the bonfires' ashes littered with charred bones covered in congealed human fat and the jewels they had worn until their bodies had fallen apart and blown away on the ocean breeze.

He followed the breeze down the serpentine streets, letting his hands brush against the concrete buildings, tasting the memories trapped within each layer of stone, each pebble of sand finding its way between his bloated toes. His breath was heavy. Each step an eternity trapped inside another until finally the streets broke opening on the vast expanse of beach that had been his childhood spreading endlessly around him. The wooly skies cloudy and dark, the sand of the beach unlike the postcards tourists had devoured, dark brown and full of the filth of life, seashells and dead crabs, carcasses of jellyfish, and to his surprise, the long dead remains of an old horse.

This must be the place. He thought, the waves tickling his toes.

He walked on. The water rising to his knees, then to his whale of a stomach, passed his Adam's Apple and over his mouth.

He caught a last breath through his nose, and the dark waters covered his eyes and head. He walked on, pushing against the current, savoring his last breath of fresh air, remembering the child he had been, the child who, despite living by the beach, had been too ashamed of his looks to learn how to swim.

He released his last breath under the waters of Yoff, the salty liquid filling his mouth and lungs. He struggled against the pain, letting the synapses in his brain slowly explode into tiny big bangs, back to the moment of creation. Leuk Daour. Khadim Mbaye. Once again one with the land and sea of the people that they had wanted to serve, and had failed.

———

(Routers) – The world breathes a sigh of collective relief.

After months of uncertainty, empty coffin funerals and international mourning, things have returned to a semblance of normalcy in the West African nation of Senegal.

Senegal had been marked off the map after a wave of inexplicable disappearances and a complete breakdown in communications between the country and the world.

After the signature of an unfair deal between oil company Total and their Senegalese counterpart Petrosen, international citizens residing in, or travelling to the country never returned, their flights mysteriously vanishing over Senegalese airspace, including two rafale fighter jets sent by France in warning. The events led to waves of protests in several major capital cities, and ended in desperation as loved ones failed to return.

As of yesterday, for reasons yet unexplained, planes were monitored taking off from Leopold Sedar Senghor international airport, carrying passengers that were assumed dead or missing.

It is yet too early to draw any conclusions. Many of the missing are still unaccounted for, but in the wake of these events, several major African nations have decided to break commercial agreements made with France and other former colonial powers, including a withdrawal from the Franc CFA monetary agreements that had tied former French colonies to the Western European country more often than not at their disadvantage.

There are rumors that the Chinese government is facing a similar backlash as African countries assert their independence from major superpowers.

We will probably never know what mysterious events occurred over the past few months, but in any case, the future promises to be interesting.

(Reporting by Svetlana Khanaeva in Paris. Editing by Jennifer Malone and Donald Edwards)

———

There was the breeze on his face.
There was the clapping of waves washing waves away.
There was the firmness of his hooves digging into the sand.

There was the smell of cabbage somewhere near.
There was the smell of a mare in heat calling him close.
There was the tear of a lonely child begging for acceptance.
There were so many things.
He walked down the beach, caught now, caught then, caught elsewhere.
There was pain, but there was love.
There was a feeling it couldn't place like an old master's reins around its neck, nudging him this way or that.
There was a sense of victory.
There was a sense of loss.
A sense of renewal.
He was a mighty beast.
He was a trampling storm.
He was a thunderclap.
He was an infant wail.
He was resistance in the face of pain.
He was acceptance in the face of love.
He was whole and yet not.
He was everything waiting to be.
He was invisible yet here.
He was the struggle of a lonely child waiting to take form.
He was what had been and would become again.
He had been a revered spirit, who now was a new one.
He was a mane blowing in the wind.
He was a stampeding breath on the pounding of a heartbeat.
He was the horse that had been a fat child.
He was he and he was him.
He was old but he was new.
He was a lesson learned and a forlorn whisper.
And when the time came, he would ride again.
Leuk Daour.
Khadim Mbaye.
He would keep them close.
He would become the way.

ABOUT THE AUTHOR

Mame Bougouma Diene is a Franco Senegalese-American human-
itarian living in Brooklyn, the US/Francophone spokesperson for
the African Speculative Fiction Society with an affection for
tattoos, progressive metal and policy analysis. You can find more
of his work in Omenana magazine, Truancy, Galaxies SF (French),
Fiyah magazine and Strange Horizons, and anthologies such as
AfroSfv2, Myriad Lands, You Left Your Biscuit Behind, and This
Book Ain't Nuthin to Fuck With: A Wu-Tang Tribute Anthology.
This is his first collection and is working on his first novel titled
Mūmiyā.